KNIGHTS END

PREQUEL III

ARMSMAN

MC CHAMBERLAIN

1

Stone
UWE Navy Personal Transport
Destination: World Caliadne

THREE WEEKS POST FALL PLANET EARTH. SPENT TWO LONG standard days at Sir Raghu Deep Space Transit Port. Nothing more than a tin can meant for freight and passengers changing ships to reach deeper into United World Empire Space. Not intended for layovers of more than a few hours. My mood is progressing from getting along to looking at me the wrong way, risking a throat jab. They herded us like cattle into whatever ships were available. No one said the term 'refuges' because that would mean the Emperor was wrong. I'm already condemned to hell according to my dreams, so yeah, Emperor, you lie. At least I got on a sort of decent military transport along with a dozen others, all headed far away from the non-existent front lines. Can't have front lines if there is no war, right? Idiots.

Our unarmed baby starship came under fire by an Empire of the Fathers' warship about an hour ago. Last minute placing the so-called universal medical symbol on the hull meant nothing to the enemy. The last so-called rumor update said EOF combat ships were randomly attacking anything without heavy escort. That came from some exhausted pilot running his billionth rescue mission. Be nice if our pathetic UWE Navy got its ass free of butt hurt for the sake of pride and, yeah, stupid civilian losses.

But yeah, what do I really care about what was going on outside, just on the other side of 4 meters of hardened titanium, from deep inside this personal military transport? Curled like a dried-out pretzel in a Navy officer's sleeping quarters, a room about the size of a closet and a private head reserved for junior Navy officers. I got into the rock-hard pillowless bed. My roommate, a ground army Major who isn't happy about not dying like a martyr on radioactive Earth, got the hammock. The fool swings back and forth like a child. I hope the damn thing breaks, dropping him to the steel gravity plates and bashing open an empty brain. I was dreaming the same thing—heads spilling brain guts—just with distinct faces of dead begging me not to shoot. So, waking up isn't that bad, even if it's cold and cramped.

"Can you feel that?" the Major asks.

"Nope," I say. I can feel the vibrations of proximity ordinances exploding near the ship's hull and don't care, so I lie. I just want off this tub. A three-day trip normally from Saturn Station to World Caliadne, that is now into day six, is taxing my saintly patience. We will get some time debt. Dunno what's worse, Major Ass pain, lack of party time, constant nearness of breathless space, or not killing anyone since leaving Earth. Talk about pent-up emotions. And the makeshift bar closed. Could have drank it dry on my own. Upside, I got to spank the pretty bartender in a supply closet. So, I am a man in need. Right? Just didn't feel all that great after all.

"I think they are hitting us with mines," he says. Like he could know. Army puppies wouldn't know a space mine if they stepped on it in space boots. Mines sit and wait for a target to get too close. Depending on the mine trigger, they don't come looking for something to blow up. Maybe he is thinking of seeker missiles. Some look like mines. Why anyone thinks projectiles in space have to look like arrows is beyond me. It's space. No air to punch through.

I try to roll over. My face is up against the hull wall. There is nothing else but unforgiving space on the other side that I wouldn't live to enjoy if so much as a pinhole opened up. Can I say spaghetti on the way out? I sigh. The hull feels cold against my forehead. Minus two hundred Kelvin on the other side. Chills the insides unless you're lucky to have an inner compartment with circulating warm air from the engines. My head aches, but the cold feels good.

I'm shivering from booted feet to head like I have a fever. No one completely understands why it's common for some to get a slight temperature on space trips. I bet it has to do with artificial gravity. We Earth humans have no idea what we arrogantly think we understand.

I bet it's alcohol withdrawal for me. The damn ship ran out of booze, the only cure, except for modern anti-hangover meds. No one has until we arrive at World Caliadne. No sign of illegal but necessary drugs either. So far, I've kept from puking or crapping like a busted damn.

Major Pain in the Mass says, "Our mass is too high. Too many refugees and cargo. Should have left the cargo behind. More people instead."

I can't help myself from pissing the Major off. "Major, who the fook cares." Keeping my teeth from chattering like those chipmunks when they get mad.

"Can't believe you, Stone. People are more important than alcohol. How the hell did you get off Earth anyway? All you have done is bitch about everything. You call out in your sleep. Whatever you did the Christ will call you to answer. Is there anyone else in your world besides you and your ego?"

I am getting annoyed. I almost punched him in the face yesterday. "Listen, Major; I don't care. We got lots of people left over. Besides, we needed culling, getting rid of the lazy and dumb. As for my world, as you call it, it is my world of one. A world you are not invited to. Not that Christ fella either. How many billions? Keep your faith to yourself, or so help me, I'll find an airlock." I can feel my temperature rising from sub-zero. It's not like he and I haven't had this exchange before. If it didn't put my ass in trouble, I would have done it. Not like it's the first time pushing someone not deserving oxygen out of an airlock. The look on a face when there's no air to breathe, no pressure for the body and zero heat to keep from freezing is so worth it.

Nothing I can do but endure until we get into orbit, then wait forever for the surface shuttle stuffed with civilians to land at a ground spaceport. The bunk shutters. Captain Asshat says, "That was close."

The man's a genius. "Probably a ship dyeing, with all the Majors on it. Lucky you are here with me."

Who knows, I may be right. Damn, EOF been dogging us with surprise visits since leaving Sol. Maybe I won't have to worry about anything soon.

The pounding persists, slow, then quicker, rising in intensity. I know that even with thick armor and at least rudimentary anti-targeting systems, these personal transports have, sooner or later, something will burn through, opening parts of the hull to hard space. With any luck, it won't be the deck I am on. Most of the ship is hanger space for troops and equipment. So, too bad for those packed in, like as Dad used to say, sardines. No idea what sardines were. Just as the space thunder started, it stopped. There is no sound in space, our minds just have to fill in the noise.

Sleep comes with its horrors.

I awake in a sweat. This time I dreamed about the jobs for Don Falcone I did before Earth fell. Except they blend like dreams do. That job that took me to dead zones in Europa. The fella, a Greek, ran from me then tried to hid in a bombed out radiated factory. Fooker glowed in the dark. Last words were on about killing some big ball official turning out to be hit on Queeny. Screwed that up really bad.Right when the mind starts to slip from deep sleep to time to wake the fook up, Selene comes floating in. Sexy as sin. She tells me about fire and brimstone and the weirdest animal called a dragon. Heard all that hellfire from Mother. Dragons belong in little girl fairy tales. I miss Selene in a way I never thought possible. And this is what normal humans do with their idle emotions?

The ship-wide PA booms on, pulling me back to reality. "Attention. We are clear of enemy ships. We were avoiding two EOF destroyers. They died by the brave actions of our Emperors' Navy with some assistance from the godless Imperium. God save our Emperor. Ship Captain out."

I feel a warm blanket fall gently over me. Selene used to cover me up at night. What a wonderful woman I let get away. Okay, I'm pissed off now at myself. How stupid can a man be?

Another day goes by. I'm down to fidgeting. Walking the alleyways meant for smaller crew sizes having to duck or smack the forehead. My anger must be radiation on its own. People move out of my way.

The food is best for dogs and cats. I bet that puppy of one Agent Saska is still alive somewhere, eating better food. At least there is water. Warm as pee but wet. Then the day ends. Days and nights get screwed up so easily in space. I avoid Major Ass the best I can.

Sleep invades like stealthy night intruders. The dreams start the instant eyes close. Are they waiting for me? Same faces, same names, same wounds, same killing hands of mine. The blood never washes away.

Somewhere deep inside my sleeping brain, a screaming

nightmare stops as if someone pressed pause. The voice of a woman pulls me away from clawing deathly hands. "The Queen is near." Sadness, like, when Mother died, sits on me like a fat elephant. An echo comes back from rebounding distant mountains. "The Queen is near." My dream voice screams back, "Who the fook is the Queen?"

The PA system crackles, popping me back into reality. Fook me; I hate that sudden shake-up wake-up. "All civilians must prepare to exit via the utility gate doors located on deck 14. Shuttles will transport everyone in order of women and children first to World Caliadne spaceports as space allows. Able-bodied men of all ages will assist in carrying cargo and personal belongings. Please be patient. Please follow all instructions as requested by crew members assigned to your section. Failure to follow directions will immediately result in serious consequences. Remember, our United Worlds are at war. Be courteous and helpful with neighbors. Demonstrate loyalty and obedience to Emperor with actions of kindness, bringing honor to our Emperor and Empire. Thank you for your attention. The Christ be with you."

The Major is there, dressed in army fatigues, sporting a sad collection of medals with little meaning. In the SAF, we didn't get medals because we didn't officially exist. Officers had markings on their sleeves, and that was it. He says all smart and parade like, "Get up, lazy ass. Maybe you could convince someone in the Anastasi to give you a purpose. You're not army material, not in my army of real men who fight. Glad to not know you. Next time I meet you, your ass goes down. Understood?"

I just nod—still a long way from the surface of awareness to think of a smart-ass reply.

He leaves like he's the Ship Captain, and the spaceport won't let us dock without his okay. Asshat. Meeting him again someday would be a good day for me, very bad for him.

I get up. Looking in the mirror, what I see is bad, pale gray, haggard. I need a drink. I need a shot of Red in any form. I need a woman.

I laugh. I say out loud in my best deep bad guy voice with a little old Italian accent, "So, Asshat Major, if you only knew who was sleeping near you for all this time has put more people in space cans to float forever, unknown and forgotten, you would suck your thumb in fear calling for your mommy."

I make some scary faces in the mirror. "Yeah, I am the badass. The best the Strategic Armed Forces ever had. They call me Stone. Dragon of Death because I spit fire. Okay, I just made that up. Hell, what have I come to? Talking to myself like a fool."

Now I feel like a washed-up, homeless, planet-less vagrant. I could introduce myself as "Hi, my name is Stone, from World Earth. Sorry, I mean planet Earth because some alien humans blew it up for us." I really stink at feeling sorry for myself. Maybe this is what it's like to wake up and find out what kind of person one really is inside.

No credit, no illegal Yen, just the clothes on my back are all the things I have. Oh, and Dad's watch. I smile because I still have 440 hidden from Major dumbass. Well worth all the sweat and worry of smuggling it all the way from dead Earth.

It takes another four hours to disembark, shuttle to the surface, deal with immigration, threaten the right people, to walk down a crowded street of lost sheep who thought Mother Earth was forever.

Stupid people. Nothing is forever.

2

CITY NEW CAROLINE HUGE 3D VIEWERS HANG EVERYWHERE, pumping out excited voices, synthesized explosions in hard space, floating 3D Newsheads, and product offers of things I never heard of. The Emperor promised to be transparent about what happened to World Earth, and for once, a righteous promise came true. It wasn't hard to figure out why. Even with a population of a trillion or more, word spreads fast with RT communications, especially about what happened to Earth. The Emperor needs someone to blame and keep the masses in check. Easy way is to show who did all the damage. Suspiciously, they play down the presence of Imperium battleships.

People stand around in groups with jaws open, eyes teared, and shaking fists at the sky like they could make contact with someone taking the blame. Kinetic weapons smash the soft face of Earth, sending mushroom clouds almost touching space. Fire and biblical brimstone, just like

Bible version 1 said. Nothing left to call home unless a planet covered with its insides is home for radiation, ten million proof fire retardant space suits. As I walk down a street looking for something cheap to drink, I see a bar sign down a long alley between questionable businesses.

Finally, a bar, seedy but has liquor, so I don't care. Inside I find the last of humanity on its final drinks. No one looks close to sober. They all look mad at someone. Seeing as I just walked in, mad at me is just fine. Give me your anger. I need to work off some issues of my own.

At the bar, I slip between two women. They don't seem to care. After all, do I not look like a near-dead, smartly-dressed Adonis Italian?

One woman late forties on my left, obviously badly colored black-green curly hair, big red lips, dressed in a smock of sorts, says, "Buy ya a drink, stranger?" She isn't bad looking. Then again, it's been a while.

"Sure. Crickets, please."

She laughs. "None of that here, sonny. Dry beer or hard whiskey."

"Today, I'm a whiskey drinker," I smile like I am happy.

She snaps her fingers to the bartender man the size of a gorilla with about the same skin and hair, then deceptively, she sets the drink down with a soft touch. I get a dirty look like she wants to say she's in charge.

I say to the bartender, "She's buying." The woman's look didn't waver. The woman on the right looked away, my guess wishing she was elsewhere, then headed for elsewhere, I think I heard her chuckle. One woman is all I rather deal with right now.

"So, you just come in from where?" the remaining woman asks.

Hours, I don't know how many later, I wake up from a pleasant alcoholic after-sex haze. The woman is right beside me, snoring as a horse should. Lips vibrating like an out-oftune violin. The pleasantness is not going to last, judging by the room smell and something furry near me.

She stirs, curling thin hairy arms around me. With a hug, she breathes day-old stink. "What's your name, big man?"

"Stone," I say behind suppressed reflex gags.

I feel crusty feet rub my legs. If she is thinking of sex, it's going to cost a bottle of something strong to dampen the stink.

"You want to know my name?"

"No need," I say. Gritting my teeth to keep from another much deeper gag from yesterday's food. Too much of whatever it was they call dry beer. The stuff tasted like horse pee. Can't let my mind go there. I need to get up.

Her hand, calloused and thick like a brick mason, pulls my head to face hers. I want to look away, but it's like headlights in space. The breath, oh no, the breath. She wants to kiss.

I felt it start. I couldn't move. No way to stop it. It was over with one retch.

The thin plastic door slams open, startling both of us. I dunno where 440 is. Fook.

The woman goes insane. Screaming like she just saw the biggest spider. I laugh. She starts hurling insults about my body, attitude, heritage, and how better sex is with a banana than me.

I put a hand over her mouth. "Shut the fook up, woman." Her eyes are about to pop out.

"There you are. You look like death. It took me a while to track you down. Should have known I'd find you in a hole like this with a thing like that," a familiar voice says, choking back snorts. Ugh, it's Jimmy.

I look at Jimmy then back at her. "At least she is legal."

The woman thing goes berserk, pulling my hand away and flailing arms around like a bird. I can't blame her. She just got puked on and called a thing.

Jimmy says to the woman who stands there naked, rather ugly, flabby belly, skinny hairy farmer burn arms, legs like little sticks, and covered in off-brown freckles under the hair forest, "Bitch, get lost." She leaves with smock in hand, muttering something about someone coming to beat my ass. Not sure If I have any self-respect and manhood left to beat.

"Hi, Jimmy," I say meekly. "I'm pretty sure that wasn't the woman I took home last night. Wherever this is, I dunno."

Jimmy waves my excuse away. "Get dressed. I have somewhere you need to go."

"Just a second," I say between retches. It must stink wicked. Jimmy covers his face.

"You done now?"

"Yeah. Where and what?"

"I need you to space can someone, like now."

Suddenly, I feel better.

3

Stone
Misfits Eggs & Bacon Restaurant
City New Caroline
World Caliadne

"Serious, Jimmy, I can't eat. Not yet. The least you could have done is bring me some NMH pills. My head is imploding," I say while trying to hide the shakes. Not sure if I could win a fight with him or a granny like the one over there giving me the eye. Normally, I'd give her a wink. Make her day.

Jimmy loves this. He says, "You mean NMH as in No More Hangover, illegal and punishable. Never would I deal in such contraband. Now, if you wanted some RedFrost, sure." His face remains serious. If I could focus with two eyes to coordinate a punch.

"Stone, you never learn, do you? No wonder they kicked your ass out of the SAF. The big badass Italian killer can barely hold down eggs and greasy bacon. How the hell did anyone trust you with weapons?"

"Don't say greasy," I say, doing a mock gag. Better not do that again.

It's like reality has teeth that just sunk into my flesh right to the bone. I look away, back at the granny. She is smiling but trying to hide it. I should just go there and sit with her. I bet she has a hundred stories that play better than the last couple of days.

"What's the matter, Stone? Did I hurt those hard feelings? You're not going soft on me, are you?"

I manage a weak smile. There is nothing inside me to puke up. A plate of three eggs, runny, thick, shiny bacon swimming in light brown grease, a slice of ham burned, something that was once brown beans, a side of barely toasted toast, all of which is fake. None of that is going inside me. Coffee is thick like hydraulic fluid, betting it's hours old. Besides all this is a tall cloudy plastic glass that holds the one thing that always helps hangovers; tomato juice. Dunno why. It just works. Not going to think about how dirty the glass is or how old the juice is. It's staying down.

"Next time you wake me up before natural body functions ring my bell and not bring No More Hangover pills, I will forget to stop beating the crap out of your sorry ass," I say. Slowly, with care to make sure no lingering alcohol slur hints.

Jimmy wisely says nothing except for that cheesy smile.

"Make it quick before I decide to go back to some other hotel to sleep," I say I say nothing about being basically broke.

"Okay, relax. Don Falcone sent me to speak with you, with what's left of you. Not going to lie, me being here is not what I think is best for the Families, but the Don sees the bigger picture," Jimmy says. He leans over, nearly dunking the old fashion necktie into an empty plate of congealing grease. "My curious mind wants to know what went wrong back on World Alacora. Why didn't you follow orders?"

I sigh nice and loud. Waving my coffee cup for some more

slurp. As usual, no one sees me. No patience for this. "Getting some coffee, don't leave. I'll find you, and I won't be nice," I say, pointing the trigger finger sign language.

"I am not leaving. Can't wait to hear the story," he throws back.

No one around, so I get my own cup filled. Too bad some when on the floor, like it makes a difference anyway.

Taking my time back to where Jimmy sits there talking to someone on his SatCell. Wish I had taken the time to figure SatCells out. On impulse, I stop at Granny's table.

"Morning," I say. Giving her my best post-hangover self-confident smirk.

She looks up. Bluest eyes ever, like deep sky blue from old Earth. Hair short, gray and white streaked curly hair, a wrinkled face but still womanly attractive. She smiles with a full set of perfect teeth. She says, "Good Morning, young man." Her accent is faint. A little like that man I met before, where was he from, ah yeah, Earth's long-gone Ireland. Yeah, Allen McGuinness. She's waiting for me to say something if I wasn't so damn messed up in the head.

She reaches out and touches my hand. Her hand is warm. Dunno why that is so weird. She says, "Your friend is looking for you."

Looking at Jimmy, he's waving impatiently. Like the ass he is, he yells across the mostly empty restaurant, "Stone, for fooks sake, the old woman is too much for you."

I ask Granny, "Sorry, I didn't mean to bother you. Do you mind if I stand here for another minute, you know, to piss that ass over there off?"

She says, "Well, young man, I can't have people thinking you are going all fresh on me. I have a reputation, you understand?" She stands up, like half my size, and swings a bag the size of a large SAF ammo pack over a slouched shoulder. I wonder what's in it, like a small tank. "I will be on my way. You are doing just fine. Before I take my leave, young Stone, a wise man called Yoka once said, be happy when looking up because there is nothing but dirt under feet."

"Huh?" I say.

She walks away. I ask, "Who are you?"

"They call me Hazel," she says. I want to stop her. Jimmy is now yelling. "Jimmy shut the fook up."

And the granny is gone.

Back in my seat, Jimmy is right on my ass. "Who the fook was the old lady? Did you crawl over her too?"

I am lost for words for a moment. Rubbing my head, I realize my head isn't hurting nearly as much. "No idea who she was. Just some old woman wanting to have a man before maggots have her."

Jimmy laughs. I hate his laugh. He says, "Anyway, back to business. You are going to tell me what happened on World Alacora. Lets recap. Don Falcone specifically asked for you to do a cleanup. You went to World Alacora, all happy to kill someone. That Greek girl you were crawling over, Selene, daughter of Antonis Sanna —that's her name, Selene—made a big fuss over you leaving her for a job. I'm thinking good thoughts like all is well in the orbit of Stone. The next thing I know, goons take me in the middle of the night to see Don Falcone. He wants an explanation that I do not have. He tells me you fooked up. I act stupid. He says you are back on Earth. I say something like, oh no. I was not at my best that night. I managed to ask what happened, which bought me a gut punch. So, all I do know is people are dead. More than asked for, which is your style. Seriously, when I say this, the Don gets a call right there and then while I am gasping for air. We are to board a private Emperor provided ship to escape Earth. I am thinking while watching Earth depopulate before my eyes, where and what to fook did you do. Personally, and do not take this the wrong way, at that time, I was hoping to the Christ you were already dead or would die soon on Earth. Obviously, I am wrong because here you are, almost dead.

Now, we get safely off Earth to Saturn Station, the Don comes up to me and says bring that asshole Stone to me. The or else implied."

"Jimmy, it's obvious. I am sure everyone knows I choked. Didn't complete the job." I say. I'm thinking more about pissing Selene off.

"Stone, as far as I am told, the right people are now floating in unmarked cans, what's left of their earthly bodies after you shot them into bits. What did you miss? Tell me what happened, and I'll fix it for both our lives. Don Falcone sent me here to personally sort this out as in one chance only." He takes a breath, shuffles around to find words. "Look, I don't like you or how you do what you do. We go a long way back to your father. Respect for the man; he saved my ass. If you have a death wish, fine, let me live. I like my skin on, thanks."

A load of kids with parents making head-banging ruckus exploded into the restaurant and my head. All happy and not concerned about the world around them. I wonder if people have already forgotten about Earth. Don't they know we are at war with aliens? Naw, the Emperor can't have panic in the streets. And here I am talking about killing, space canning, our own humanity for fun and profit.

Who the hell was that old woman anyway?

"Okay, let's get real. The Don could have killed me anytime. I don't hide that well. Why would he want details? Why would the all-powerful Don want to keep me alive? I have a hole to crawl back into until they find me and skin me alive." My hand finds 440 under my arm, hidden by what used to be a very expensive stylish sports jacket. If Jimmy screws with me, he dies. Maybe me next.

"Alright, get your hand off the gun. Look, we were a team. Now I am back at the bottom of the list for everything, which means you are right there with me. Your coattails worked well for me on the way up, not the other way. Hate me. I don't care. Before I end up in the torture chair, how about what happened? From the moment you stepped off the liner to do the job."

"Heh," I say, "It was a good time fight." Totally unable to hold back a satisfied grin. For the first time since I opened my eyes, my head is clear, my guts don't burn, and even the cold food looks good. Straightening shoulders, folding hands like my Dad did when he went into relating his fun times, I start the story. "I got off the shuttle on World Alacora and stepped right into a firefight. It was, as Mother would say, a blessed moment."

4

Knight Rogan
Battleship Tarragon
1109 Light Years from World Caliadne

"Rogan, my love, please do not worry so," she says, using her pouty frown. How marvelously I have fallen in love with this princess more and more every day since we met in those ancient forests of our home Doragon.

My forehead creases from worrying too much these days and nights, leaving behind haunting lines. My hands ache from gripping Vanguard's sword strapped to my side. The medical people say I have a malady called arthritis. Unlike damp mornings back in Doragon forests, our apartment on this starship is metal cold no matter what we do. As small as the starship called Adona is, I like her better than this starship made for war, not creature comfort. For as chilled those mornings were on Doragon, nothing can compare to waking to songbirds, the crispness of forest under boots, and Sienna's long deep breaths of warmed air.

I say calmly, "This warrior does not worry, my Lady. I prepare my mind to defend the Queen Princess with all my heart." Placing my cramped on Vanguard's sword hilt, I declare, "And her father's sword."

She giggles into a broad smile. I love her smile. I love everything about her. The long amber hair, drawn into a braid down a slender bare back, small shoulders that carry the weight of a Kingdom. Eyes, those eyes of molten amber, liquid love for me to drink as wine from Doragon fields of fall grapes. Beauty far more than a mortal man I should dare enjoy while worlds around us fight for freedom. But why do I dread my days?

I say, "Smile always for me, my Lady, my Queen."

"Always, my Knight, dressed in Doragon leather armor," she giggles. "Rogan, please reconsider your uniform. Again, I ask you to think of how my council views Our military leader."

"Rorena, please, not this argument again. You know how I feel. This so-called uniform is who I am. A man who serves the Queen and Kingdom, slaying dragons in space. I've always been an Armsman. It is true I carry the rights of a Knight of Doragon. I am an Armsman at heart, a servant of Doragon first and foremost. This is how Armsman dresses to serve the crown. I cannot change tradition."

She slowly shakes her head, eyes tied to mine. I can tell what she will say next. "Rogan, you were the last Armsman; now you are the last Knight of Doragon of my Kingdom. Please, oh please, step into the armor with the Tarragon crest. At least the chest plate. Do you not understand all Imperium sees you as a Knight championing our armies? These people we are to meet need to see who we are. They think of us as nothing more than bedtime stories. Did you not read the history material given to you by Our Ambassador McGuinness? The history of Earth's humans, so filled with bitter war, spiced with peace. They believed in princesses and kings at one time. Read about the stories of dragons, brave knights on four-legged creatures called horses," she pauses to laugh, "as if those animals could match our Sienna."

"My love, I consumed every word. These Earth humans are nothing more than one step away from barbarians," I say firmly. She knows I do not like these people. They cannot be trusted.

"Rogan, do not tempt me. I shall become your Queen for a moment to move your loyalty."

I can tell she jests, but a part of her is serious. If she and the council, especially the man of death called Theran, had their way, they would dress me like that man, Admiral Edison. My medals come from on the scars of battles I led common men, Dragons, and Knights of Doragon.

She kisses me unexpectedly. Hard. I do love the way this woman can make the entire universe disappear. And to think, all my life, I believed there existed nothing more than a planet called Doragon. Long gone, Doragon.

I remove the chest leather armor in favor of a pretend metal I do not understand. It is not made of Doragon's hands, yet it shines silver, and in the center is that dragon we all revere, Tarragon. At least I am allowed my sword—her father's sword. Now, my love smiles, warming hearts without a word.

We attend the Imperium Council meeting. One hundred twenty-six worlds represented by my Lady, my Queen, the Sovern head and body of our Imperium. At the table: Admiral Edison, his aides, eight others with various responsibilities, Lord Theran, the mysterious and oldest man alive, and the strange speaking man called Allen Monroe McGuinness, Ambassador to the UWE and father to Princess Eden,, the Imperium Queen's sister-adopted sister but I wonder about those mysterious strings Rorena attempts to explain.

Then there is me, the so-called General of the Imperium Army. I'd rather be on a world surface somewhere, anywhere, doing something dangerous. I lead men, but not these men with weapons I do not understand. They tell me I should carry a hand weapon that fires not arrows of Doragon hardwood with iron tips but metal objects that can tear a man into pieces. I have my sword. What else does an Imperium Knight require to defend the love of his life, Queen Princess Rorena? Life was much simpler as an Armsman walking the forests of Doragon with my best friend Sienna in search of dragons to kill.

The meeting is long, wordy, with many pictures made from devices I know nothing of. They talk of fleets of warships that belittle the Doragon's Solan Navy. The once-proud Solan Navy, with its fifty-some cannon-laden sea ships, did not survive, yet they fought bravely without hesitation when the call to arms came. I always miss my friends, all of them. These men argue about methods and strategies. No one asks me. I am happy they do not. My experiences with cavalry and foot soldiers cannot compare or compete with the likes of Admiral Edison and Lord Theran. Our Imperium forces are nearly back to original strengths, they say, just as when we first entered this distant star container they call a galaxy. My mind cannot understand the distance they speak of nor the way time does not obey the movement of stars over the new worlds we claimed under our flag. I am but a simple Armsman of Doragon in my heart, still dreaming of where my next dragon to slay would show itself. No, I must not say that. I am but a simple Knight of the Imperium. For my Queen, I will stand beside her as the last Knight until my name is no more. Please, stars above, grant me the honor of giving my life for my Queen.

They speak of the Imperium's rescue of World Earth, or perhaps in truth, the failure to save the world from destruction. Never will anyone live there again, as I am told a fancy word called radiation will eat the flesh of a man before a taking a breath. I was not there. My Queen requested I stay with her to give her council. I know the true reason. Of what use would this man from forests know of space war?

We watched from our safe distance in comfort on devices that showed in amazing detail what occurred to World Earth. My heart grieved as so many innocents died. A world destroyed by Hate. It is not the first time my eyes have seen this take place, but I do wish, with all my energy, it is the last.

I remember the moment I saw a harmless starship filled with innocent people escaping Earth, a freighter it was called. I remember how my Queen stood, her eyes wide, a hand pointing, and how the room vibrated with her powerful energy. All I do know is this universe I do not understand is somehow connected in ways human eyes cannot see. My Queen, a slight of a woman, born of royal blood on a world compared to Earth's medieval ages of swords and Knights, wields swords made of energy that powers forces far beyond space and time. Who am I in all this? Just a man in love. Just a man who would die for his Queen and the love of his life.

The council meeting concludes. Lord Theran, Ambassador McGuinness, Princess Eden, and I stay behind to speak in hushed tones. My Love is playing safe politics, as she learned at the feet of her father, King Vanguard. Oh, how we could use King Vanguard's wise and powerful, sometimes ruthless hand.

My Love says, "What is the location of the Earth human we wish protected."

Lord Theran speaks up, "The man we speak of is safe, walking freely on a United World Empire world called World Caliadne. His exact location remains unknown. It is difficult to obtain information from the government and religious sources concerning the man. I must declare I have little use for religious structures. We do note the man enjoys his life's path and that of alcohol to lessen discomfort in such I have grave concerns."

Allen quickly adds, in his rolling accent, called Irish, "Aye, that it is, mate, a fluid provided by unknown gods. As my daughter will swear to." I ask him to repeat as the device given to me to translate was slow with his accent. He smiles and slows his words. He does well working with us, given he is the man looking inside at our different ways. Here I stand in garb that his people think only worn a thousand years past on Earth. The good man has won our admiration by adapting to Doragon ways without complaint or, worse, looking down upon us as if we are lesser.

Princess Eden, my adopted sister, frowns her displeasure. She speaks fluid Doragonian when called upon. The Queen and I are pleased with her adoption of Doragon as her heritage. "Yes, Dad," she says in his language, eyes focused on her father. They do have a complex relationship, from what I gather. My Queen adores her. "Father, remind me not to challenge you again. Especially Uncle Theran. "

Lord Theran just nods his wise bald white head. His eyes never change from death black.

Allen coughs. "I have stories that prove otherwise." Lord Theran looks away. Sometimes I do like this, Allen. Lord Theran was once my enemy, now my friend. A man I have fought to a draw. My respect for him is as wide as these stars are apart.

My Love sighs. "Focus, my friends. There is much to do, to prepare. Our future and that of the United World Empire, all of our combined humanities depend on these plans we weave."

Princess Eden asks, for once without her typical disrespect, "How, Sister Rorena, will this excuse for an Earthman help us? I don't know his name or what he is that makes him special to us. Yeah, Uncle Theran, before you gloat, I know you know more than Dad and me and my adopted brother

Rogan, standing over there grinning. I get it with all these mystical mumble power energy love-hate connections, but isn't it time we knew more?"

I must admit Princess Eden is as hot-tongued as a dragon breathing fire. Yes, I do love the young Lady just as a sister. She had a hard childhood she endured, especially at the hands of fanatically religious women of Earth. We have talked into the night of our lives. I would protect her as a sister I never had.

My Love raises her hand to stay the talk. She says, "I will tell you this. The man I have selected is a man of powerful hate. His heart is made of my father's castle walls, thick and unmoving, strong and loyal. The life of another is not a concern for him. Only that of himself does he care. A man highly skilled in the complex arts of war in these worlds we now govern. He has a weakness that is a hole in the middle of walls, a missing brick if that makes any sense. When he sleeps, the flood of memories that haunt him returns. Princess Eden, my dear sister, in our studies, what does this mean?"

Princess Eden isn't one for on-the-spot testing. I can feel the apprehension. She says, "Sister Rorena, please do not test me in front of my friends."

My Love's face turns dark red. The air in the room feels hot and smells of burning wood. Prince Eden looks at Lord Theran, then her father. They know better than to interfere. Princess Eden has much to learn, all of which I am not privileged to know. My heart, they tell me, is not large enough to house the powers of Love. I wonder if Hate would fill my heart.

A long time crawls past like a wounded creature seeking help. My mind drifts back to when the battles for Doragon involved arrows, swords, shields, and fire-breathing creatures we called dragons. I must never forget the barbarians. Where would our Imperium be this day if it were not for their mad dedication to slaughter any enemy daring to challenge them?

From what I have been led to believe, this man we will allow to carry our banner must have Barbarian blood ancestry.

Finally, Princess Eden says, "Fine. Sister, have your fun. The nameless man has a good heart under the bad stuff you call Hate. Give me a break; the nuns and sisters didn't teach this in Sunday school."

My Love smiles—a good smile. She says pleasantly, but I know she is exhausted, "Princess Eden, for your sauciness, you shall sit quietly to calm your attitude for as long as I desire, and I do desire a good time pass for you to think. Take your leave, please. Lord Theran, if you please, I am tired and require rest. Kindly take Our Ambassador with you to inspect the fleet arrangements with Admiral Edison. I fear the dear Admiral's anger may cause harm over subordinates we need to keep."

Princess Eden snorts like a pig my father and mother kept at our home on Doragon, the pig we eventually let go of because Mother felt sorry for it. Lord Theran and the Ambassador bow, then leave me with My Love.

"Are you okay, my Queen?" I ask.

"Yes, of course. I needed to end all the talk, especially of this man we seek to have our hand over."

"I must ask. I know it is not my place, my Queen. Is he a threat? The mysterious man you wish to keep alive?"

She sighs deeply, not from my questions; it's from the endless pressing wall of Hate seeking a break in her defenses. I cannot see these threats because I am not aware. Without hesitation, I would place between Hate and her Love. She says, "Very well, my dear Rogan, my Knight of my Kingdom. The Armsman who saved me from a dragon. Look at you, so formidable. I am always safe with you."

"Have I ever let Tarragon live that down?" I say playfully. "No dragon of Doragon bested me. I saved the princess from being eaten," I say, snapping my teeth mimicking hunger.

She playfully shakes her head. Her hair has come free. I

cannot refuse to entangle my hands. We kiss long and intensely. I can feel her drink my energy. Please, my love, drink all of me. Let me die for you. Give me a purpose.

She whispers in my ear, "The man will become an Armsman in due time."

I frown hard at that. She says, "Do not fear, Knight Rogan, you will always be my first and last forever and ever. Who else saves me from dragons?"

We kiss again. We hold each other. I cannot imagine my world without my lover. If I could live forever to protect her, I would live as a happy man.

I do not know why, but I must know. I ask, "What is his name, this soon-to-be Armsman as if a lowly commoner man of Earth could become a Doragon Armsman? Tell me his name so I can challenge him to see if he is worthy of Doragon honor."

She presses a warm forehead to mine. Her eyes, red from lack of rest, stare up at me, looking for my strength. Dear sister, I desperately wish I had more to provide. She says, "Rogan, this man we speak of is a man with no honor. You cannot challenge him. You cannot see him until the time is fulfilled. He will hate you and me and not care to see the reason why. But I know what he wants. I know how to turn his anger into power. We shall do all that is impossible, then more, to protect our people. My people. I am disgusted by the man's presence. I wish there were another way. No one can know of this."

Then the thought occurs. "Rorena. Truth, please. Was this man you hid from me on that starship fleeing Earth's destruction? The man that so many of Admiral Edison's fleet gave their lives?"

She says nothing. That is my answer. I nod in understanding.

She says, "I love you. Yes, you were the last Armsman of Doragon and the bravest of them all. Now, my love, you are my Knight, the last of a grand line since time began for our lost world Doragon." She looks away from me to hide tears. I wipe away those tears of a Princess as I have many times before.

I guess, in a small way, I do have a purpose

5

Stone
City Ashdod
World Alacora

So, there I was, sitting in a washroom in Sir Trenton-Ashdod Spaceport. In a stall, standing on the toilet seat, wondering if the fooking thing was about to fall apart, dropping me into the stench of hours-old crap. The worst part was the wrong washroom. Women's only washroom. And women were screaming the way scared rabbits back on Earth did.

SAF didn't do many missions in heavily innocent civilian populations. Dead bodies of people who had nothing to do with targets bring eyes no one wants to be involved. Nothing worse than a Grand Investigate Dedicated to Truth. In other words, bureaucrats with dull knives stab anyone unlucky to take the blame rather than the innocent Emperor. True, on a few occasions, a certain news organization mysteriously lost a few newsheads in deep space. No one followed up on why that happened. One of my SAF buddies said once after he just put down, as in killed, several mission innocents, stated everyone is guilty of some sort of sin. The women trapped in the washroom and those outside in the hallways ducking behind anything solid to avoid death from repeater fire all have sins that they answer for, just not that day and not by my hand.

"Could all of you cry-baby-hysterical women calm the fook down? I got this. Okay? I can't hear what's going on outside," I said loud enough to get the point made while notifying everyone outside I was stuck in the lady's room. Not the best idea.

It took a few seconds for the last whimper to fade away. Now, I could hear distant screaming mixed with loud, angry voices coming from the hallways outside.

Looking up at the ceiling, I can see the main light system for the washroom. Intelligent light systems usually have a central pod that talks to the rest of the room, shutting lights down when not needed, adjusting the air, etc. I said, again just loud enough, "It's going to get dark. No one screams or says a word."

Waiting for a few seconds. Took my silenced 440, aimed at the pod, and popped it. The lights went out. One woman let out a weird sound like a yelping dog.

Pitch black. Space black, like no sun, moons, or starlight. What I would give for Dead Man's Eyes the military grade see daylight in darkness field glasses. Slowing breathing slows the heart and keeps hands from jitters. SAF trained us to let adrenaline do its thing as long as we control our response. Fantastic drug. We often used it on missions.

I didn't know how long I had before the bad guys came looking. But I knew they would. They didn't have forever. Sooner or later, Anastasi assholes would show up, see the last batch sent to find out what was going on were dead, and also see a number of innocents laying around bleeding, dying, being dead. In that mix of blood, four dead bad guys already dispatched to whatever they believed in. That was my doing.

No one will kill me that easily just because I look like I'm half asleep from a boring space shuttle trip.

Question was, how many more hostile guns were out there?

Footsteps of pretty boy shoes echo the silenced washroom. No one breathes. I knew whoever owned the shoes would look in each of the five stalls. Of course, I was in the last one. And the other four had at least one person sharing.

I had to get the bad guy to me first.

"I'm down here, dumbass," I said, kind of cheery-like.

The shoes tip-toed to minimize an echo. The man tried not to breathe heavily from uncontrolled adrenaline. It's all about the timing. We put people on planets light-years away, yet washrooms still work the same way. The door to the stall wasn't locked. It started to move inwards.

The next question was, is the owner of the nice expensive shoes smart enough to stand to one side or right in front of the door? I didn't wait to find out.

The three-point shooting tactic. Left to right, or right to left, depending on current surroundings, then two in the middle. I go with one in the middle, then left, then to the right, but not too far, being in the end stall with the wall on my right, then one in the middle again—all quick, as in pop, pop, pop, pop. Just in case, I pop three more at random. Pretty hard for someone on the other side to dance out of the way in time. I heard a grunt.

I stepped out of the stall and almost fell over the body. One more educated headshot location pop ended any more noises other than a last exhale. Not bad for just about no light.

I heard a couple of muffled woman-like sobs. "It's okay. Bad guy down," I said.

Made it to the washroom exit in the darkness without crashing into a wall. Listening there at the door returned nothing more than a whoop-whoop warning siren. Someone in power had taken control of the spaceport. Time to get out before getting caught.

I said, with a sincere tone, "Good work, all of you. Stay where you are until good people come. Have a nice day."

Some woman said, "Thanks for killing them. Now, fook off," then after a thoughtful pause, she added, "Please."

I said, "My pleasure."

That wasn't the end of the day. Body count so far at five. Got me one more on the emergency exit. Rat like fella. Tried to kill me with a ridiculously long knife. I put it in his head right down the middle. Talk about a splitting headache.

Body count six.

Upside for me was the confusion of hundreds trying to get out of a complex not meant for that sudden traffic of terrified sheep. I blended in and found my way to a side street with a bar. Are they not everywhere in the God-fearing Empire? Sheep and bars?

I went directly to a worn pretend leather bar stool and ordered a rum of any kind, downing it before the bartender walked away. They have thrown me off my game. The bartender is a five-footish, firey red-headed, pretty thing dressed in farmers' overalls with no shirt under the top half. She had a bunch of pin-on buttons that made some sort of joke, a few that blinked. The best part of the bar right there. She wasn't that old looking, maybe late twenties with the still fresh unworn look and plenty legal. Very important that part.

She turned back to refill my shot glass, and that's when I took note of her staring meant something more than welcome to my bar, you sexy Italian man.

Eyes can talk. She poured another shot, her eyes abruptly shifting to the right as if something important in that direction suddenly appeared. Down the drink goes, the glass smacking back to the table, hinting at another. She pours another then her eyes go to the left just as abruptly as the right side.

I ask, around the glass to my mouth nice and quietly, "You served?"

She casually points a slender neon-painted fingernail hand to the whisky bottle while nodding yes. Some odd brand of whisky, but that wasn't the point. It had a full-color white sail sailing ship from Earth that had cannons used in very different wars. She served in the Navy, most likely in an officer position. I figured something so slight as her didn't get physical with the fellas. I was wrong. With the free hand, she made a secret finger sign known around military services, three fingers pointing instead of the usual one used to mimic a weapon. She served as a Marine. Wow. That took things up to atmospheric levels—good fellas and ladies, a bit of an ego bunch but no bigger than mine.

Two bad guys, Triads, smartly sat apart from each other, which gave cover for the other if someone came for them. Too far away to get my hands on directly. To many others in the way. I go for one, the other jumps in. Smart plan. Triads are formidable and smart, unlike rush in weapons blazing Russian Family style.

She said like nothing was wrong, "Pay up when you're done." I'm struggling to keep my mind focused. The overhauls with no top shirt take my mind on a sailing boat ride elsewhere. She goes to the other end of the bar, pretending to clean up.

What to do. Felt like a stalemate.

A viewer above the bar, a quite nice one, at least 75 inches of passive 3D, had the local football game running. A newshead interrupts with reports about a shootout at the spaceport. Video from security cams shows chaos in the hallways and gates. I knew what came next. My hand went to my concealed 440 under the jacket. Never wear a stupidly expensive light-colored jacket. I noted a few blood splatter spots. Annoyingly hard to get out.

Jimmy interrupts my story. "Stone, the Triads got wind you were coming in to take out a prime target; what's his name? Chang Jin, that's it. He was the target to get rid of, preferably quietly. I don't know the details, but something to do with black trading with the EOF bunch. No one knows how they found out about you coming for them. You didn't get captured, which would have ended in a bad experience for you, so good for that. You took the heat from the Anastasi wanted list. How many times for that illustrious listing of your sad Italian face on how many billboards and SatCell screens? Stone, you have become a pain in the ass to clean up behind. Anyway, Don Falcone pulled strings to get you off the wanted list by paying off the right officials. Where is this story going?"

"Yeah, no kidding, they knew. Those bastards don't screw around. Full war mode right in front of civilians with security video recording. Someone in the Families close to the top set me up is my theory. I am betting some soon-to-be-prisoner civilian with an illegal video device was recording the whole event.

"As much as I appreciate Don Falcone getting me out of the Church Anastasi hands, why bother? He's out for my ass. Could have had me easily killed in any prison here or on any world."

"Because Stone, he wants your ass unblemished by inept Anastasi for his own ass-kicking. You disobey orders. Didn't they teach you that in the SAF? What I don't know is why you didn't do what you were told. Kill Chang Jin. Putting him in a space can either for real or symbolic. I assume this story will tell me why. Then maybe I can fix this rift between the most powerful Family head and his least reliable shooter."

"You haven't had the privilege of reading my profile. I do more than shoot," I say with pride. Making myself sick, thinking I'll owe Jimmy a favor. "Anyway, I like telling my heroic stories, so shut up and let me go on or fook off."

He does the ever-irritating eye roll.

———

So, there I was in the bar, about ten others there minding their own business, with two Triads having orders to kill me and anyone in the way. Either they got lucky in finding me there or followed me. No matter, they needed to die, just not the innocents.

Do I use the unsuspecting citizens enjoying a drink in a little bar on a cloudy Monday afternoon as a wall of protection, or do I risk myself to get them out of harm's way? The viewer on the wall made the decision for me. A full-screen facial of one handsome Italian shows up with a caption: Wanted for questioning. Do not attempt to engage. Call local authorities @111 immediately.

I'm thinking, maybe dangerous? No, I am dangerous.

Silence. Word does spread fast in a bar. Lots of frightened looks. People left like the building was on fire. Me, the brave bartender, and two Triads remained.

Who moves first? I didn't need to spin around the barstool to look behind. With all the people gone, a mirror cluttered with various bottles of multi-colored liquors and hard photos of nearly naked women reflected what was happening in the bar behind me. Yeah, I was hoping one picture was the bartender. The Triads knew I could see them. And they sported self-satisfied smiles as wide as their little faces could produce.

I turned around on the swivel seat. I said, with glass tipped, "Drinks are on me, gentlemen."

One of them would most likely get me. Question was, which one was fast enough and accurate enough to hit and kill because unless I'm dead, I'll fight until I am.

The bartender speaks up, much to my surprise. She came close, pouring my glass full. She said, "What service?"

"SAF," I said.

"The Christ, you say," she said.

"Yep. Got any cannons on that Galleon?" I asked, hoping she got the idea.

There is a pause, then it hits her, "Yeah, I do." Nice smile. White teeth like real ones. I had to wonder what she was doing in that bar.

I slowly spun around on my barstool, the damn thing making the worst noise like someone never cleaned them. Out of the corner of my eye, I saw the bartender on my right messing around with a bottle that didn't need any messing around with. She was waiting for me to make a move.

For tactical sense, I designated the right side Triad as Mr. Right and left as Mr. Left. The bartender was on the side of Mr. Right, but he didn't seem to care about where she was. He would shoot her after me, and I think she knew that.

Mr. Left gets up and slowly draws a small handgun. Nothing like 440 in power and range. Mr. Right just sat there with a blank look. Maybe he felt scared. I am nasty-looking.

I said plenty loud enough, "My body count is six so far today. You two are seven and eight."

Mr. Left took aim. Slow enough. I could have walked over and taken the baby gun away. He was sporting an I win face and body swagger to match.

Did I know if the bartender had the balls to do anything? I could only hope.

Mr. Left came within three feet. Perfect distance. He said, "You die, b-a-ss say so. First, we hurt you 'cause you kill friends."

I said, "Your face hurts me. Your lack of standard English hurts my ears. I think you mean boss, not b-a-ss. Are you a product of sheep sex? Your pale brown suit hurts my sense of fashion. How could you do any worse?"

That threw him off. And like all dumb, poorly trained asshats, he waves the fooking gun like a stick, pointing where I need to go.

Bang. The sound of an old-fashioned sawed-off shotgun is a marvelous sound, especially when it's not pointed at me. It fills a room with reverberating waves of pure weapon sex. Too bad for the receiver of the shot. Even at that distance, Mr. Right will not find his ears, nose, or lips. I need not look. The bartender is my new friend.

I went off the stool a little wobbly; damn swivel threw my leap off. Mr. Left pulled the trigger before he re-aimed it at me. Didn't know where the shot went, didn't care at that moment. Taking the little baby gun from his hand, easy with a grab and twist with my free hand. I still had a shot of whisky in my right hand.

He had to kill me or die. He knew it. I had to kill him or die, and I knew it. Strong motivation. The thing is, I am trained to do this with anything in hand. I let him hit me twice in the head to give him the feeling of victory. Felt like a fly. I said, "That's the best you could do?"

The bartender probably would not want to use that glass again. Can a man beat another man with a shot glass? Brains make a mess. Got that gray-red stuff on my light-colored jacket. Waste of a decent Italian made jacket.

"Are you okay," I asked my most favorite bartender. She stood at the end of the bar, still holding the shotgun leveled at the faceless Triad. Kind of interesting how the dead body still sat upright. A little blood still squirted upward.

That's when I spotted where the stray shot from Mr. Left had landed. A growing river of bright blood ran down her tanned arm right where a colorful tattoo of Poseidon glistened.

"You're going to be okay. Nothing important. Just a good story to tell your girlfriends," I said after checking the wound.

"You SAF are balls in spacesuits," she said. It's a compliment. I always like it when females talk about balls and space.

"Naw, I was ground mostly, left the floating to the space boys. Good shooting, by the way. I bet that ordinance was augmented for distance and thump." She nods a wink to that.

"I am guessing you worked officer line work. Nothing on ships."

"Marine all the way, SAF wanker. Fireline for me. I ran the heavy weapons. Lobed the heavies hundreds of miles on dickheads. Got my hands dirty."

"Wow. Okay. Impressed, I am. Anyway, glad you got the heads up on the ship type. My dad loved wooden ships from like the 18 hundreds. I gotta leave. Someone certainly has called Anastasi for their blessings."

I could tell she was about to introduce herself and her probable heritage back to 18 century navy days. I said, "I don't want your name as much as you, and your skills crank my interest. Thanks for your help. Someday I'll return the favor. Call me Stone."

I left out the back door. Anastasi assholes everywhere, but I got a ground taxi, one of those illegal transporters everyone pretends is safe, and went directly to a motel I had already picked out using a few Yen and a fake name to cover. Amazing how a fat slob manning a motel counter will look the other way for a few Yen and a glimpse of my 440.

Jimmy interrupts again. "Really? I'm surprised you didn't try to bed the bartender or kill her."

"Body count going up. Eight isn't a good number for me. Besides, she saved my ass." We both laugh. Him at me, me at him for laughing at me.

"Okay, all of that is news come and gone. Can't you get on

with it? So far, other than a public gunfight in a spaceport, a shootout in a bar, nothing out of the ordinary."

I'm lost in thought. It's obvious. Jimmy asks, "Are you going to puke? You look whiter than usual for an Italian."

"A little spooked. Wonder how that granny I just spoke to knew my name. Am I that famous?"

Jimmy just rolls his fooking eyes.

6

Stone
City Ashdod
World Alacora

JIMMY AND I LEFT THE WORST RESTAURANT EVER TO WALK DOWN a street filled with truckloads of kids with attitudes. Even saw a vamp or two. That is just the tip of the empire iceberg of weird people. I pass a holo advert jumping out at me for World Gamora. Very suggestive girls and guys were dancing in a lurid way most church members would shy away from. My kind of dancing to watch. It won't be there long before some heavenly thinker has it removed.

"Now, there is a world that panders to the underbelly of everything the Church is not. It is the center for all things humanity has to offer in the way of sex, drugs, and terrible music. This Alacora is a bright white snowdrop compared to World Gamora. I so need to go back to Gamora one day."

"You should die there. Perfect place for you," Jimmy sorts back like he is funny. I ignore him.

"There is a shopping mall down the way. Decent walk for a few minutes in fall weather," I say.

"You Earth mutts get so up on the season crap. This world has one season. Chilly and almost always raining. I hate it here," Jimmy moans. Not much about this guy I like anymore. "Explains the fooking huge bugs bug people get all excited about."

He has no idea what bugs are. Some worlds have ones that are as big as dogs. Evolution has its own agenda. Of course, the Church says it's just God expressing his creative talents.

"Stone, I assume you have more to tell me about, exactly why you pissed off Don Falcone so bad he wants to hang your skin on a wall beside dead animals he hunted down. I know you did not complete the job, just not the why. We have a ten-minute walk. Go."

"Sure. The best part to come," I say.

Back at the dumpy motel, I regrouped. I knew the job was on the rocks, but you know me, it gets done one way or another. Showered, got something to eat, pounded down everything I found for water, then called a ground taxi.

The cleanup job, if it could even qualify for a job seeing as my presence was now known, was to take place at Mitchel apartments just outside the main city. Upper-class district just over the bay. No way my target would be there waiting around; I mean, you know the hitman is on the world you are on. Do you stay at home counting money?

And all I had was 440, silenced, with four clips left. Lots of shots, but I wished I had more variety. Oh well. Do what I do with what I got. Once saw Dad send a man to hell with a coat hanger, or was that the time with a pen?

Cutting to the bottom line here. I went to the address in

hopes of a lead. Took me a while to get a hand on someone patrolling the outside grounds about as inconspicuous as waving a flag. Walked right up behind him then kindly helped the surprised fool to a nearby park seat. 440 in the kidney is convincing. He babbled in Triad talk until I put the 440 where men don't like a gun pointed. He gave up the super-secret hideout for target Chang Jin and his father. I didn't care where the father was, just Jin.

I shot the useless guard through the armpit. Couldn't have someone spoiling my surprise visit. His body just sat there kinda slumped over, sleeping. I dunno, may still be there, with some flies or whatever eats dead people on this world.

Body count nine. And the day wasn't over.

Now I knew where to go. Across the city to a meat processing plant. It turns out this backwater world is known for its pig exports. Every imaginable thing one can ask of a pig.

By the time the sun goes down, I arrived at the piggy plant, paid the taxi to forget me, then spent a half-hour scouting the outside of a single large building. Big place. Lots of oinking.

Not one look-out guard other than workers in white coats doing whatever men in white coats do in a pig factory. I saw a couple of men in shorter white coats with pink hats. I figured they were in charge. The place was full of pigs and lots of automachines doing the heavy lifting work. Getting inside came easy. Walked inside through the delivery door along with a shipment of new pigs. Friendly oinkers. The autobots just ignored me. But things got interesting from that moment on.

Pigs stroll in on four legs, then end up coming out in packaged parts, so there are not too many people around to run the show. Found a white overcoat, a little short for my 6 feet, and a soft pink hat. I looked ridiculous, but with the pink hat on, I belonged in a fast food place with kids. From that point on, anyone not in a white cover is suspect. With a SatTab, I had no idea how to work it. Walking around looking important went well. All the other white coats ignored me as if I belonged. After about ten minutes, a man without a white coat strolled by like he owned the place. Trying to hide a long weapon under a small coat didn't work, and eating what looked like a cooked piggy leg, all yelled I'm a bad guy. And lucky me, he leads me directly to a built-in office-like structure up against the plant's back end wall. Hideout found. One door I could see. Two large windows lined the outer office wall. Shutters closed from the inside kept the inside private. The whole structure looked like it was made from some wood and concrete block.

I hollered just before the pig-eating man opened the office door. "Hey." Then a friendly wave as I approached, showing the SatTab as if something he needed to see.

He turned an ugly, angry face. I think he told me to fook off in Chinese.

Body count nine. Need more.

Picked the dead pig-eating body up to face the door. Good thing he was light but a lot shorter than me, so I ducked down just enough to peer around the dead man's head. At least he smelled of aftershave of some cheap kind and not pigs. I banged on the door, hoping there wasn't a knock code. The door opened to the surprised face of another Triad bad guy. He said something in complicated babble. I said, "Catch." He did pretty good.

Could I have planned this entry any more screwed? My patience was gone into space. I needed a drink badly. First time in a long time, my hands shook. Not bad enough to ruin aiming a hungry-for-pig 440.

Two shots into the bad guy opening the door. Stepped inside, straight to the knees with my 440, gauging office space targets. Time slows for me. It's the advanced training SAF drills into the head. No idea how it works or if it really works. It just seems to work.

The moment of truth or death.

A frowning old Chinese face, glossy eyes wide, skinny as death, sat at a desk. I assumed it to be Chang Jin. Two more Triad armed targets needed to go down quickly. One about a meter away approaching the door. The other at the back was aiming a repeater. In the middle of the office space, sitting on a metal chair with gray-taped arms and legs, sat a naked woman, bleeding from a swollen nose, lips, and one closed eye. What broke tactical focus was where fingers should be, only blackened stumps remained. Where toes should be, only blackened stumps remained. Where nipples once were, blood trickled. Her legs were spread open to display something only the truly sick do to a woman.

All that I've seen before. Never surprised. Until I recognized who the woman was. The Marine from the bar. She spotted me. For a second, she had hope in one eye.

I think it was the old Asian that said, "No kill."

A booted foot took my 440 away to land almost outside the office door. Not good for me. Up on my feet to block the next kick. A kung fu chest punch puts me on the floor. Damn, the little guy had a powerful punch. I tried to get up. Back down from a pistol whip. Most people would be down and out, a captive at that moment. For me, the titanium plates rang true. It hurt my brain, sending a shock wave, confusing my eyesight for a moment. Upside for me, the Triad looked a little upset his pistol handle didn't do a clean head crack. Tackled him into a flip over my head. He landed on the hard concrete floor headfirst.

In one corner of my eye, I see the repeater center, ready to cut me down like a tree. The old Asian, Jin, was on me like a young man. He Kung fu-ed my Italian ass. Landing on the still unconscious first Triad broke my fall. So far, my nose was broken and bleeding like a broken dam, maybe a rib or two out of alignment. The bastard kicked my knee hard. Definitely, a limp for a few days if I survived the fight.

"You no get up, white man no good fight," Chang Jin said, inside condescending laugh. To the man with the repeater, he pointed and said something about tying me up onto another metal chair.

"You enjoy pain? I give you a present; much pain. You wish call you Christ, you do. I allow."

SAF gave us recruits plenty of training on torture. How to give and to take. Didn't like the taking pain part much. SAF also trained many diverse forms of martial arts for situations. Getting up with a squishy body isn't easy, so I played wounded floundering fish. No way I was going into the chair.

The Triad fella sweeps the repeater behind his back and reaches down to grab my hands to tie them with a length of plastic wrapper I bet used to hold pig's feet together. All this time, I look just enough through eye slits adding lots of verbal moans for effect. Chang Jin is babbling along about a Chinese story of whatever. All I cared about was he was preoccupied. The only other sound is the bartender Marine making suffering sounds. The mind, in pain, sends orders to make noise, even if the person is unconscious.

Just as the Triad fella touches my hands, I dart both my hands, one set fingers curled at the middle knuckles (my fingers, broken and rebuilt with strong unbreakable bioplastics), into the fella's throat, while the hand I did a Y into his buggy eyes. Blind and unable to breathe, the Triad stumbled away, falling into the bartender. Jimmy, that, I tell you, takes strong fingers and practice. Try it on you sometime.

Jin swore in standard English. As much as my knee hurt, I got to him before he could deploy his handgun. He didn't expect me nor see the incoming uppercut. I had only seconds before the old fella would counter.

The race for 440 was on. Even though no one else could have used it with DNA protection on, she still made for a nasty weapon to bash a head. I wasn't going to make it in time. Bartender marine saw and acted. Dunno how she managed it. Maybe it was the Triad falling on her that loosened her feet enough to tip the chair and her body forward. I can only imagine how much it hurt, or was she far from feeling pain anymore? I dunno.

Chang Jin tripped over her. He lost control of his gun. I arrived in time to get my beloved 440. Looking back at a red-faced Chang Jin lying on the hard floor, blood trickling out of a head gash, made my day, maybe the entire week.

In five minutes, I tied him up with complimentary pig feet ties. Two barks of 440 made sure neither Triad boys would interfere.

Body count now at 11. Still, about eight hours left in a long 27-hour day.

Chang Jin sat in the chair meant for me. As for the marine bartender, I took off the restraints. She collapsed onto the concrete floor. Chang Jin decided to yell. Can't do that very well with a pair of soiled panties plugging the hole.

"I can get you help," I said calmly to her. She wasn't entirely with me, kind of like on a surface existence. Her body and mind had to deal with serious trauma that most simply could not live through. The Triads are known for torture, usually done quickly compared to Brazilians, who love making it last for weeks. Dunno why the thought of how nasty the EOF is with their pain technology I heard, can last for years.

"No," she said, trying to wag her head and eye to make a point.

"I can't save you. You need professional medical care," I said. Looking her over revealed the extent of internal injuries caused by men with no respect for a woman's womanness. I am a womanizer, but not an abuser like that. This was wrong. Someone had to pay.

"Let me go," she said slowly, carefully making sure I understood.

"Can't let you suffer, Marine. You will be in agony before the end." I said with real respect. "I can get you help."

She moaned. "Send me on my way, please," she said clearly. No doubts about the words. She tried to grab my hand, but without fingers, it didn't work well. So, I took her hand as best I could.

She said, "Name is Lieutenant Lisa Havenworth."

Looking into a nearly closed red eye that still tried to focus like a camera Dad used to have that had a bad auto-focus, I said, "Lieutenant Havenworth, thank you for saving my ass. I'll take care of you, Lieutenant. SAF Respect."

She tried to smile a thank you. She died quickly with no more pain. Not counting her death to my daily count.

"Chang Jin, I am going to make you feel really bad. She was a good person. Why did you do that, for fooks sake? She had nothing to do with me."

Chang Jin was trying to tell me something. I took the panties out and said, "Talk Standard English or in this goes."

"My name not Chang Jin," he sputtered around sticky, chunky throw-up.

I wanted to say sure you are. Something in his voice, face, and eyes made me pause. He kept looking to the back office, where some boxes stood almost to the eight-foot ceiling.

Someone was hiding there. If it was a bad guy, I'd be dead long ago. Chang Jin wanted to yell, but panties stifled it to a muffled yell.

What did I find behind the boxes?

A kid, about ten years old, maybe eleven. Asian features. Long hair, glasses like a techo-beaker, skinny but not in a bad way. Dressed well enough to suggest a well-cared-for child. Who brings kids to a pig factory, let alone a torture session?

Something wasn't right.

I put a bunch of packing tape over the kids' eyes and ears.

Too bad about the hair getting tangled. It didn't take long for a box knife to encourage Chang Jin to speak the truth.

Jimmy puts his hand on my shoulder. We just got to the mall. I hate shopping malls. I hate shopping unless it's handmade suits for me or weapons to go with the suits.

"Wait a minute. Are you saying what I think?" Jimmy says behind a face somewhere between surprise and disbelief.

"Yeah, you're smarter than you look."

We end up in a little coffee joint. Good, more coffee. Black, hot, and syrupy strong.

Jimmy orders us a coffee of some wild name and accessories to put in it. Coffee cups with low-end scrolling graphics are kind of fun to watch. I just wanted a simple coffee.

We sit at a table at the back. The shop is full of teenagers. Boys with one thing on their minds, and girls just wanting daddy's attention.

"Yeah, I was supposed to kill the kid, not the father. I assume the name for the wrong body."

Jimmy sits back hard. Looks around like the solution is there on the back of one of the kid's neon sign jackets. He says, "You didn't do it."

"Nope. Shot the old man instead. Okay, truth, I made him suffer some more. The kid didn't see anything. The little fella didn't struggle. I took him out of the office, found an employee, and had them call the local Anastasi detachment. With a gun in your face, people are so happy to call anyone for help, even the Church's bullies. They came and arrested me. Didn't care. I guess that's when the Don got me out of jail. When the Family lawyer came to check in, I told him I killed the kid. I guess the Don found out later I lied."

"That explains it all, then. You let the kid go. The Don

didn't let you go, as in being free to run away. He just wanted to kill you himself."

Jimmy leaves me to make a few calls on his SatCell. I wish I knew how they worked. He comes back looking sheepish after like 30 minutes of me fending off cute 16-year-olds trying to ask me if I am single. Meanwhile, jealous boys are wondering if they can put me down. The way I feel. Maybe.

"You going to turn me into Don Falcone?"

"I explained the story. Highlights anyway. He was still pissed. The kid was meant to balance something the Triads did to a high-up Church official's kid. I got him to agree to one chance, mostly 'cause of the innocent girl, the bartender. She didn't deserve that. She was a vet and apparently decorated for pulling in several of her people. It turns out one of the ones she saved was a cousin of some guy who knows the Don. Anyway, she did good by us. You didn't do good. You're just one lucky fooker."

"Not going to do the kid. I don't care why a kid got marked at that age. Not his fault someone else fooked up, a Church official at that. Let me guess; it's one of those divisions that don't allow marriages let alone kids. Anyway, as soon as I could, I grabbed a liner back to Earth where I knew I could hideout. Too bad Earth ended. Nice timing or what?"

"Stone, shut the fook up. This is darker and deeper than space politics you wouldn't understand. Just say yes and do the next job, and don't screw up. All is forgiven. Just don't forget I talked Don Falcone into using you."

"What is the job?"

"A certain government official needs to go down. Trust me. This is your only way back in. Do this right, and you will live. I put my reputation on the line, or what's left of it? Before you say it, yes, I have one left, and yes, I will get paid well."

I learned a long time ago not to trust Jimmy, but what else could I do?

7

Stone
City Ashdod
World Alacora

Jimmy left me sitting here in this stupid mall, surrounded by kids who have no idea how to dress with respect to look nice. Why wear nothing that matches, of every known color, oversized and undersized, with odd-looking media devices attached to places where bodies were not designed.

Now I feel like crap. No way I put down a kid, like anything under sixteen, and even then, it better be a mass murderer, sex offender, or something undeniably evil of Satan, so the Church says. That little kid will never be normal. I'll never see him again, I hope. Not my problem.

I am to sit here to wait for instructions. In this bad excuse for a coffee shop. At least it's warm. At least my face isn't on the news feeds anymore. Don Falcone has lots of clout. The news about a shootout at the spaceport is now presented as an exchange between Imperium agents. That just seems like bad galactic politics. I may never understand or care about high-level negotiations involving fleets of spaceships and armies of mindless soldiers, but I do understand staying alive. I need a drink. I need a motel, a woman, a drink, and maybe just a quick shot of RedFrost in any form.

Sitting with my view towards the front of the café. Anyone comes in sporting that telltale look of "I am looking to shoot Stone", I shoot first. At least my back is to the wall where the washrooms are.

A hand lightly taps my shoulder and sends a chill up my spine.

A female voice says, "Are you not curious, Stone? What happened to the puppy?"

I keep my hand on 440 under the jacket. I say, "Well, well. If it isn't Agent Saska." Not going to ask how she snuck up on me and wreck what's left of my pride.

She walks past me to sit across the little booth table with a trailing scent of flowery perfume. A little strong but much better than a burned coffee smell. She isn't a bad-looking woman for a baby manufacturer.

"Stone, how are you? I see you made your mark here on this little civilized world."

"Saska, how not nice to see you. Unless peeing in the men's washroom qualifies as marking my territory, I know nothing about any mark," I say with a pretend concerned look. She does a mock chuckle then stretches her arms like surrendering. She dresses in an off-white, somewhat frilly shirt that magnifies amble chest muscles. No idea what else she's wearing. Loving the ponytail. Her eyes are a little Asian, looking more than I recall back on the freighter when we escaped Earth. Fine with me. I can't be sure if she is armed, but I best prepare for that.

She yawns, puts elbows on the table, face in hands. "Didn't think Mr. Jimmy Chan would ever leave. You don't like him, do you? The look on your face is worth a picture or two, but we already have them. Surprised to see me?"

"Yes, and no. As for Jimmy, he is just a friend from a childhood long over. Unless you have something to say important and quickly, I have a motel date."

She says, "No, you don't. You have no other reason to be here than to visit the moon above. I'll get to the point." She sits up straight. Hands went out of view. I wonder if she noted me moving silently to unholster the 440 sliding it under the table. Under table shoot-out, western style.

"I am not here on official business. You are not in any danger here. So, put the 440 away quietly. Let's not do anything stupid. We will get up just like a couple of friends just finishing a coffee and leave this dive. My car is outside in back. I have a safe, quiet place to talk. You want to talk to me, right?"

Decision time. I could just shoot Ms. Agent Ponytail, leave, and move along to another dead-end path. Or see what she has to say. How do I know this isn't a trap Stone plan? Put Stone in jail somewhere no one knows about, then hang Stone into a giraffe neck?

I don't know. But she is good-looking. And I can go down shooting.

"Well, let's go," I say.

Out the front door, around an alleyway to the back. Typical dingy garbage collection alleyway. Keeping my eyes open for anything suspicious. Shoot first mode for me. Keeping her one step in front.

The car, she says, is what Dad called a rattle trap. No sophisticated electronics. Uncomfortable seats. Dirty as a pig's pen, and I know more about pigs than ever.

She says, "I have a safe place nearby. Keep your mouth shut until we get there. Pull your 440 again, and I will leave you on the side of the road with or without a bloody wound to die slowly. Understood, Sergeant?"

I sit up straight, giving her a modified salute. "Yes, miss," I say. What else can I say? What I want to say is keep talking to me like that and risk a good spanking. Maybe I'll hold off on the smart-ass stuff.

The motel we end up at is middle grade—nothing important to attract attention. Just two people, a stunningly handsome man, and pretty decent-looking woman, settling into a room. No one would care.

And yeah, it's a plain jane room. Nothing like I enjoyed only a while back working for the Italians.

"Are you with me, here and now Stone, or off on a mind trip from too much Frost?"

I say nothing. The chair near the window faces the door. Best I can do for a view of the room. Second floor with no balconies, so no one is coming in the window. Time for business.

She takes off the half-cut overcoat. I think it's an agency issue. The white shirt is tight, with her a little overweight. That's okay by me. Women making babies the old fashion way can cause body rebellion. Now I notice standard agency black pants, partly comfortable, partly tactical. She is a field agent at least some of the time. MIS Field agents are much better trained than most departments. Maybe I'll get a tussle with her, see who's the better.

"Look at those tactical shoes? Is that a set of pink lips on the top, over the toe?"

"When someone stupidly says kiss my ass, I can kiss their ass," she says. Her hand goes around to reach for a gun, I assume. She goes slow. Outcomes a Lagerfelt 50. "Nice weapon. Good range, reliable but small mag. Only 32 shots."

"It works when I need it," she is now purring, the command voice is gone. She is starting to look like a decent steak, not the best, just the right size for a filling meal.

"Relax, we have a lot to cover. Drink?"

We drink out most of the pathetic room bar.

She tells me about the baby and a little girl I didn't know about. All good, she says, then changes the subject. She focused hard. Good. I still wonder what side she is on, MIS UWE loyal out to trap me, protect the Empire from a disaster, or maybe the Family has something on her. Time to flush the information toilet.

"Who am I going to can?" In my mind I recall the image of the radiation fella I put down. "Wait a second, that fella dying from radiation I put of his mystery. He was on about a hit. On Don Falcone, right?"

She goes quiet for a moment, looking around to find the right words written on walls with bad paintings of ducks. She says, "How much of the war news do you understand?" Her voice is back to command mode.

"As much as needed. The Imperium are kind of on our side, against the common enemy Empire of the Fathers, EOF for short. Acronyms everywhere, right? EOF took out Mother Earth. The Imperium intervened then retreated to a line some 900 light-years away from UWE space. The EOF are farther away, behind us, so to speak, in space, leaving us in the middle. How's that?"

"Technically correct. What about the faith?"

"Faith? You mean the Church and Emperor? I assume without listening to newsheads, the Emperor has his right-eous nose out of shape over having to acknowledge other humans besides us. I've heard enough of rhetoric. Earth humans are the Christ's chosen. EOF and Imperium are subsets. As far as I know, the Imperium is not God-fearing. Bottom line; a couple hundred million refugees from where we do not actually know other than they followed the EOF here."

"You have the cleaned story. The Imperium are not Christians. Period. The Queen, the official leader, refused to acknowledge the Emperor as the government and leader of the only Church. Our Church and faith come first. As for the EOF, they are beyond any comprehension of understanding from where our Church and government sit. Our Emperor has classified them as demons, straight from the bowels of hell. A bit dramatic, I agree. For clarity, it's more like just between 1 and 2 billion Imperium subjects. They like to keep that intel secret. EOF are twice that size perhaps more. Nothing as large as our UWE. The last census a few years ago put the population around 5 trillion, give or take a billion. One would think population rules. Stone, you can understand this, technology rules. The Imperium and EOF are far past our levels."

She pauses to finish off a small bottle of low-quality vodka. I think she is a qualified drinker. Makes me happy.

"So?" I say, trying to play stupid.

"So, think a little bit higher on your pay scale. The Imperium leadership is the bottleneck. We need to motivate change in thinking. They must understand who we are. Superior. Period."

Getting bored of the narrow-minded political talk. She looks far too enticing, laying on the bed, head up with all the pillows. "Get to the point, Saska. Who is the target, or should I ask how many are in the target?" I say with all intended frustration.

"Okay, I am getting to the point. I know this; certain officials in the Imperium and UWE, nameless at my level, recognize the difficulties with her, the Queen, and her immediate, trusted counselors. Without that difficulty, powerful people in the Empire feel strongly better relations are available for all concerned."

"Yeah, I get it. Access to technology past what we have. The combined weight of our military and theirs would be the trick needed to send demons back to hell." As I say that, I realize how plain stupid it sounds. Mother believed in hell, hell, she lived in hell. Dad did too, but he embraced it as a good final retirement destination.

"Exactly," she says. She was up off the bed, slinking over to me. I can still smell the perfume.

"Say it, Saska. I need to hear the words," I say. She leans into me, puts hands on my face, looks into my eyes. She whispers as if she fears her own words, "We want you to do your patriotic duty for the Empire and Emperor. For the Christ. There is a plan to eliminate a high-level official in the Imperium. It is a mission that one retires from. Are you interested? Think of never working for the Families, or anyone, ever again. It is a yes, we move on or no, and you leave, never to see me again."

I'm thinking high-level in the Imperium isn't Don Falcone. Hiding my disappointment. Maybe another time Don you sadistic bastard.

She unbuttons my shirt, which I don't mind at all. I say, "Briefing over for now?"

She kisses me. Hard. Like she hasn't kissed anything male that isn't in a diaper and under eighteen for a long time. Do I mind? Hell no.

Well, that was good. Naw, really good. She was like a wildfire and me the extinguisher. Hanging on to the ponytail was a new idea. I ordered pizza. Kids still deliver pizza with pizza faces driving junked grounder cars with someone's girl giggling in the passenger seat. The pizza is good though. Got some watered-down Lopsi, basically sugar, with more sugar and some sugar flavor with a shot of fizz. We had a few laughs at who could burp the entire alphabet.

Watching her sleep feels good, just like Selene. Selene and I spent many days on a rented Catamaran, all of 159 feet of boat, booze, food, nakedness, sex, all on a bath warm Mediterranean with access to a private beach. Not hard to get used to that. But I screwed it all.

• • •

Saska roused at almost six local time. "How long you been watching me, Sergeant Stone?"

"Keeping an eye on you, MIS Agent," I say.

She is looking for me to answer. I say, "I'm in. What's next?"

She checks her timer then frowns into deep furrow lines. "It's time to get briefed," she says. All playfulness is now gone. "Get dressed. We need to meet our contact."

Would she have tried to kill me if I said no to the mission? It may have ended in some weird kinky sex first.

8

Stone
Garbage Collection Lot
Parish Ashdod
World Alacora

WE SIT OUTSIDE A DINGY GARBAGE COLLECTION BUSINESS. IT'S almost noon, and the maximum overhead heat is making the garbage stink. The place is closed, something to do with an outbreak of web disease. Anyone with any sense knows MorteVirusH29 is one serious sickness directly connected to previous Satanic Plagues, so says the Church that never lies I think people need to stay out of garbage surfing. She assures me it's a cover and nothing is going to happen.

We get past the traditional warning lights and tape and concrete divider barriers. A couple of security guards appear, take one look at her ident, then disappear. Garbage management never changes; we just make more of it.

"Wish I had a badge," I say like a stupid five-year-old wanting to be a crime fighter. Saska just makes a half-hearted who cares grunt.

We end in a back parking area for large hauler ground trucks. Garbage consisting of anything imaginable piled everywhere, including barrels of sludge, just another word for sewer collected from public and private sources. I can smell the insides of those cans sitting in pink sunlight for days—a very bad smell. Every possible perch has weird-looking shiny blackbirds making noise, just like crows back on Earth. I don't have enough shells to kill them all.

We stand still. Not talking. A figure rounds a pile of rusted containers used for inner system shipping. A man, a wide blackish hat like business fellas use, gray overcoat pulled up as if it's raining, and big ass dull black boots up to the knees. Gotta be a weapon under that coat. Interesting complete face mask, not like kids wear that have videos playing, just all cloudy grays. About all I can see for features are a set of big droopy ears.

"What's up with the mask?" I say, making sure my hand remembers where the 440 waits to answer a call to action. The stranger abruptly stops mid-step.

"Shut up, Stone," Saska says. "And take your hand away from your gun. This man has the intel we need. He has gone to great danger to speak."

I heard my dad say something like a tingling sense of danger about a spider or some bug. Mine was ringing tingling bells all the way to New Roma.

"No way on the mask. Full disclosure or I'm out," I say and mean it.

Silence, except for hungry squawking birds feeding on garbage.

Saska says to Mr. Mask, "Up to you."

A voice scrambled by a VoiceBoxSyn says, "Mask stays, or I am gone." The voice sounds like opening tin cans with a dull knife.

Saska looks to me. She says, "I'll have to call Jimmy and

let him know it's a no-go. It's been nice to screw with you, Stone."

I say, dragging out a stupid groan, "Give me the intel, but I am going to need assurances that it's solid. Anyone can make stuff up." Maybe I should threaten him, maybe let it go. I need to do this job to get back on my feet.

Before Saska could speak, Mr. Mask says, "We know who you are, Stone. We know about you and your past in the Strategic Armed Forces. What we require from you is the talent of getting this mission completed without any compunction. As I review the details, you will understand our reasoning for tasking a professional as yourself. A professional that does what he is told without moral issues. Do you understand?"

"Yeah, but first, before you go on singing my praise, who the fook are you?"

A long pause. It feels like the face behind the mask is looking for direction from somewhere or someone listening in. Mr. Mask says, "My name is unimportant. What you will know is I am an agent for the Imperium. My allegiance is to Lord Ungar, a man with great powers. Lord Ungar covertly represents a small but dedicated faction within the Imperium. Our common enemy, the Empire of the Fathers cannot withstand a concentrated force of our two branches of humanity. You will and must trust what I am informing you. Agent Saska is further proof of our intentions. Many have already given their lives to bring this mission to the next stage. There, does that satisfy your needs?"

"I don't give a fook about the politics or who is having dirty sex behind the curtains. All I need is the who, when, and where," I say.

"These are the basis of our choice in you, Mr. Stone, your lack of concern for politics and emotions. Getting the mission completed is what we wish from you. Your target is Queen

Princess Rorena of the Imperium. Needless to say, yet I must, this action is of the most secret level."

I say, in justifiable shock, "Wait a minute. Say again?"

Mr. Mask says, "Will this be difficult for you, Mr. Stone?"

I don't pause to answer. "Couldn't care less."

Mr. Mask laughs out loud, scaring more blackbirds into crowing. He says, "I am a patriot to my people. There are many reasons behind this decision, of which you have indicated acceptance of knowing details. As you may have concluded, knowing makes you a liability until the mission is completed. To quote your own words: who, where, and when. I have informed you of the who. I shall divulge the remainder of intelligence required to complete this mission of galactic importance."

He goes over the details of the how. Saska would assist me with any support issues, supplies, or whatever. Plan the job. Do the job. Runaway forever. The runaway part consists of a clean set of travel anywhere documents, passports, lots and lots of clean credits, and a choice of retirement worlds within Imperium-occupied space. Pretty close to being Ghosted by any Church or government eyes. I would never work again. Maybe it was time to dry out and settle down with a normal life. He also assures me the Families will leave me alone. That alone is no easy task. The Families never forget, especially Don Falcone.

"Okay," I say. Talk about a limp wiener reply. Well thought out and simple. What the hell have I gotten my dumb ass into?

A loud ring of a SatCell goes off, spooking Saska and me. For all I know, Mr. Mask didn't change his facial expression. Who hides behind a mask anyway? Someday, I'll have that mask off to kick the face that owns it.

Saska fumbles out her SatCell. She says, "I have to take this; give me a minute." She mumbles into the SatCell while walking a good distance away from where Mr. Mask and I stand. Awkward moment. Am I supposed to talk about the weather?

"So, you think it will rain?" I ask like an idiot.

"Silence. There is a loose end you must perform once the main objective is completed," Mr. Mask says. He steps in close as if I am suddenly deaf. He tells me. I ask for a repeat just because I can't believe what he is asking. He says, "Pay attention; I will not say this again. Make this final action occur directly after the completion of the main target. For your Empire and for your own, as you Earth humans like to say, ass."

"What happens when I do everything? Am I a loose end?"

I think he's smiling, given the muscles around his forehead and ears wrinkle. He says, "No. We are the true Imperium. We do not do away with those who faithfully complete missions for the good of the Imperium and your government, the pitiful UWE. As for the loose end, that loose end has many risks attached, risks we cannot reliably control. You will trust our judgment or return to the threats you face. There is no negotiation. Will you have a problem retiring the loose end?"

"No. I'll do what you ask. The queen and. . ."

I hear Saska approach babbling apologies about nothing important, so I shut up.

"Sorry, Stone, are you two done?"

"Yeah, completely."

We notice that Mr. Mask has walked away, disappearing behind the tall stack of multicolored interstellar containers. Ironically, I notice the containers all have the expression "In the Emperor we trust."

"And all this time I thought I was going to be famous. The guy who kills the Emperor. I'd laugh, but it isn't funny."

"You will be famous in your own mind. That good enough?"

I just laugh this time.

Saska purrs something about having to work together will involve more motel time tonight if I have the strength. I agree with her. Sex is like drinking; I can step up to the bar anytime. It might be a little distracting, knowing I will have to eliminate her. No loose ends, Mr. Mask says. Fook it. If she goes, he goes too, if I get the chance.

We leave. It ended up being a pretty good night.

9

Getting to World Sanctuary, where the heart and soul of the United World Empire heart beats, isn't easy with heightened wartime security. Just about every structure, statue, and old Catholic Archives, along with all other denominations revered works, was moved a hundred years ago. More statues, buildings, and churches for all subject denominations were built for the purpose of illuminating the glory of the worldwide bureaucracy that governs most of the Earth's worthy religious beliefs. Worthy, meaning knee bending to Empire hierarchy without questioning the Christ's chosen divinely appointed man; Emperor Thaddeus.

Ask if there is heightened security and get denials. No way the Church or government admits to fear, especially as it sees the Imperium and EOF as godless sub-human creatures that the Christ allows to test faith. Can't have the population thinking any time kinetic bombs could fall.

The entire world population is dedicated to one purpose,

the service of trillions of Earth humans, thousands of worlds, and themselves. Not that there isn't some redundancy spread around. A tough war lesson learned a century ago during the wars to end wars. I wasn't alive to fight in the religious wars. What fun that would have been.

Being the head world of the Empire, the Earth-sized planet has space forts the size of small cities in orbit, each filled with space-trained and rapid deployment space forces, squadrons of space-atmospheric fighters, and other useful toys. The planet's surface has a standing ground army of over a million service men and women, along with thousands of special Emperor guards called Praetorian, after the Roman equivalent. A space station the size of Sol System's asteroid Eros sits 20 thousand miles above Sanctuary, overlooking the entire system where the Home Navy Guard hangs out. The exact number of warships, from fighters to massive dread-naughts, Titans, and total personnel, is a super secret. Could have used all that firepower when Earth came under attack. No mystery why the EOF took out Earth; moral victory for the bad guys.

Within this official force, several organizations exist for various purposes, like the Ministry of Internal Services, of which Saska is a member. If she were found out, her treachery would then get the attention of the super-secret strong-arm black coat ODS, which stands for a bunch of sneaky hyper-loyal spooks that have license to space can anyone for what-ever reason they think may hurt the UWE. Those assholes are a step above the Anastasi. At least Anastasi has limits.

Boil it down to Anastasi security with eyes everywhere. They get you; you will die, sooner or later, slowly as they can drag the process out.

How I got the proper clearance and cover documents came from the skills of MIS Agent Saska. Explains at least part of her talents. Other talents include a decent sense of humor, tactical skills, and a nice-looking body.

Good work, Saska.

Looking again at my temporary papers just to get me on the World past security. Not liking the name Jonathan D. Smith, a salesman for a company that deals in plastics. So common it blends in, I guess.

So, here I am, in a not-so-bad hotel, on a business trip cover, waiting for Saska to show up. She is masquerading as a SatCell executive. She gets the nice-sounding cover. I should be ashamed. I can't wait to get all personal and then talk about work. I haven't asked, nor will I ask how she gets her information—assuming it's via Mr. Mask. He needs to die just because I said so. I'm not a traitor but me first, then country.

The knock on the door always startles me. 440 in hand. Saska has a spook bypass key. Aiming as the door pops open, just in case she isn't alone.

"Jesus, Stone, put the weapon down. One of these days, you're going to twitch and have to drag my body away," Saska says.

"Don't worry. I'll bury you deep. How much time do we have?" I ask, sporting a good-sized smile. "Sorry, I'll make sure it's a pretty can and personally launch your dead canned body into space."

"You certainly do know how to turn a lady on."

A couple of hours later, I open my eyes to see Saska lying there looking at me. "How long have you been thinking of how to kill me," I ask. We are both birthday dressed. Vulnerability isn't my strong suit. Being killed naked is an uncomfortable way to go.

She gets up, obviously irritated by my question by the way the toilet lid bangs down. From the washroom, she says, "If I wanted you dead, you'd be in a space coffin already. I do not get my hands dirty, either."

I stop myself. This conversation I want to have will wait for later. I want to kill her. Really, I do. Maybe later. "Glad to hear," I decide to say. "How about the mission's nitty-gritty details."

She calms down and is now back to being professional, although a little difficult to focus on with her milky white nakedness. She covers, arms over chest, shrugs, then sighs. "Can you please look at me, not my chest? Pay attention, Stone," she says. She isn't kidding.

"Okay," I moan like a teenager on his first sex outing.

She explains what will happen starting the next morning at 8 am local time. She tells me this must be up close and personal because it will make a perfect statement of intentions, not done impersonally with a long-range kill shot and almost tactically impossible with so much parameter security. She assures me that all elements will be in place to provide the opportunity and escape path for me. As sure as she is about my escape, I wasn't born on a solitary moon. Helping me get away does make sense, rather than discovering who I really am, causing serious issues if I talk. No, they will get rid of me after the mission is completed, so I'll shoot first and run away like a scared rabbit. At least whoever is pulling puppet strings will try to get rid of me. I'm pretty resilient, like bloodstains on white shirts. As for Saska, I'll do what they ask after I feel safe and have money to disappear forever.

So far, I haven't asked any questions about her personal life. Like kids and anyone else in her life. I don't want to know. Bad enough I know her name. Does she know what's waiting at the end of tomorrow? No, that's not the real question. It's more like, will I be the well-trained, heartless professional? That remains to be seen.

"When you leave here tomorrow morning, check out as if you, Mr. Smith, are returning home. Burn his papers immediately. Take these with you. Congrats on the promotion, Stone. I'll wager you always wanted NCO status."

I look at the new identity papers. "Hey, my name is Prime Sergeant Walter McGovern, Special Protection Services, World Sanctuary Division. Yeah, NCO means I can fook up guys without reason, just for fun."

"The encoding will show Prime Sergeant McGovern is authorized to use lethal force as required and always has a sidearm. A side of your choice. Of course, that damn 440. You should be happy about it."

"Dare I ask how deep the story goes?"

"No. The less you know, the better. The story is as complete as it needs to be. We took measures to make sure poor McGovern got the rest he so wanted. Take the disbelief off your face. I have a contact with incredible talents and patriotic loyalty to the true human race."

"Tell me the name. Whoever it is will be safe if you and I are safe. Call it a safety marker."

"I don't think so," she snaps back.

In a half second, I close the space. 440 in hand but not targeting anything. "Listen up, I been playing nice. If you get compromised, who do I contact? I can't reach the mask fella. So, who?"

She hesitates. She looks into my eyes to see no hesitation on my part. "Okay. He is an implanted EOF agent. I do not know his name. As a backup provision, if I go down or anything else goes wrong, he has the ability to contact you for debriefing. Seriously, there is nothing else I can tell you."

I wiggle 440.

"Stone, think for fooks sake. How many people in an op like this would know who is who. Compartmentalized."

I smile. "I wouldn't shoot you. Wanna have sex?"

That rattled her world.

She slaps my arm pretty hard. "Fook you, Stone. Don't scare me again."

"I'll try not to. Let's move on. With my newest identity, I head to the proper Anastasi station there, then fit in like we are all friends of the Christ. Sounds good. Other than I despise the Anastasi. Stupid bunch of fanatics with little decent training other than quoting Church rules. What happens next?"

"You will follow the delegation once they arrive at the meeting complex from the back landing. There will be a distraction. What that is, I am not informed other than it will be obvious. Once you take care of business, others will assist in causing more chaos. Make your speedy escape the way you came in. I will be nearby at a closed construction site down the street. It is vacant, so there is nothing to worry about. As high level as this meeting between Imperium and UWE is, none of the other military services, such as nearby regular Army detachments are on alert. Don't ask how that happened. Should help you to realize a lot of important people are involved up and down the chain."

"Copy that. Pretty simple, I think. What could go wrong?"

She leaves in the middle of the night after more slipping and sliding around. Glad I don't have to clean this room. After tomorrow, I will have killed, assassinated, the Imperium Queen. I'll go down in history, not that I care for that, or more like Prime Sergeant Walter McGovern will get the blame. If he isn't already dead, he will wish for death. Assuming I live, I'll see the results of a united war front against those demons of hell. Stupid thing to call them demons of hell. I don't care. I do my job. I don't apologize.

I sleep with dreams of demons from Mother's imagination that haunted her whole life. No wonder she snorted, smoked, and ate RedFrost like candy.

10

Knight Rogan
Aboard Adona
Geosynchronous Orbit
World Empire Sanctuary

"Rogan, my Knight, my love of life, please consider Lord Theran's sage advice. We are walking on uncertain ground we do not control. We must show an innocent face, a face needing their sympathetic protection. Yes, my love, I feel your words of anger you wish to speak over Earth's human arrogance. Our Imperium sacrificed good men and women to save their World Earth. Please do not forget Our purpose of most importance that dreadful day. If it were not for Emperor Thaddeus's foolish reluctance to request help, our forces could have saved more lives, not only one man of fleeing billions. The destruction of Earth at the hands of the Empire of the Fathers' hate reminds us all of how our beloved home-world Doragon died. Those evil, hateful half-men have no regard for any path other than their thirst for that they can never have. How wonderful it could have been, my love, to have saved Earth from itself and achieved Our purpose forward.

"We hope a friendship that exists only in thin words of this morning will be long-lasting words bonded with a common understanding of who Our Imperium and Emperor Thaddeus of the United World Empire must battle in the years to come. For two are greater than the one. Many of Earth's humans do not see that Our peoples are equals. Many do not wish Our presence. The Father's Empire is more than Our Imperium can defeat on its own. You know that as clearly as I. We must have The United World Empire beside Our ships of space. You know and understand all this, my love."

She softens her singing voice. I can feel words battle my resolve. "Please, for me, my love, wear the special metal fabric body protection our thoughtful friends have provided. If you are called upon to protect me, your body will act as a shield of Doragon. Yet, my Knight, my last brave Knight of thousands before you, many of Our men in arms surround your Queen, suffocating Our presence. Today We shall walk in humbleness, showing trust for Emperor Thaddeus.

"Our valiant Lord Theran, will he not fall upon burning stars to protect his Queen? Please, my love, allow those who do what their loyal hearts must do. Stand beside your Queen. Walk with me at my side."

My heart sags from the weight of duty of a Knight, the last my kind. Should a mate or Knight shield the love of his life. Who has the honor of death?

"Rorena, who am I? What have I become? Just a figure on the arm of the Imperium Queen," I say. "Shall I show fear? No one will dare bring harm on us, not as this man protects the Queen."

I can see her anger brews like dragon fire. She speaks constrained words, "Rogan, you are my mate, that is foremost. You are my Knight, the last of a kind. You are my right hand in this collection of worlds we, you and I, freed from the Empire of the Father's repression, beginning with Our humble World Doragon to hundreds of freedom worlds. You fought for me when evil Barron Ungar threatened my honor. From the surface Doragon to these new worlds, we, you and I, side by side, battle for hearts lost. I love you, my Knight. To go on without you. . . if anything happened to you. . . my grief is unimaginable. I am your Queen of the Imperium and Princess of Our Doragon. Do as I ask."

Her words are hard and burn like dragons' breath, more so as she speaks with her royal person. Yet, I cannot leave behind my past, of who I am. Who I was. "My mind is set, my love. I will carry my sword - your father's sword - just as thousands of Knights before me carried a sword to defend our way of life. As the last Knight - the End of all Knights - I shall wear humble leathers in respect of my days as an Armsman of old. And, yes, love, I shall wear the special protection underneath my leathers where none will know. Yes, I will itch, which you will promise to relieve the discomfort after all this pomp ceremony today."

She shows her heart by smiling. There can be no other in all stars anywhere with as many smiles as my love does. "I am pleased. You look handsome as always," she says, pulling me into her arms of perfection. In my heart, a kiss lands like the gentle love birds of Doragon. I only wish I could return the same. I will always be in awe of the powers my Queen possesses.

"Rogan, please know you are important to me, to the Imperium, to Our cause. Everyone on the council respects you for all you have done. When the time comes, my dragon warrior shall lead Imperium armies again in the sky, between the stars, and on the land of all worlds. We will prevail over the Father's Empire in patient time."

My head nods. My heart does not believe. I am a man

from the past. My father told me when it is time for a Knight to set aside a sword, arrows, or dragon lance, then do so with honor. Has my time come? I live in a time of war far beyond my understanding. We battle with weapons at distances farther than any arrow of Doragon.

She speaks cheerfully, but her body energy is like a mother with many children needing love and attention. I say, "And you Queen Princess, share the load of governance with your sister, Princess Eden. A level compromise, yes?"

"Yes, yes, dear sister Princess Eden is preparing for a future at our side. She is such a difficult young lady. I see many gray hairs on her father, Ambassador McGuinness's wise head. Perhaps mine, too, one day will gray with worry and age."

"Sounds like a young lady I found in the darkest forest of Doragon. An independent daughter of a certain King Vanguard," I say slyly. She is rarely impressed by my attempts at humor these days.

"Now, no more talk. We must exit this cramped ship of the stars you and Theran insisted we arrive in and enter a spaceship called a shuttle to land on the world they call World Sanctuary. There We shall find Our Ambassador Allen McGuinness and Princess Eden waiting at a place they call a spaceport. We shall travel in special horses called automobiles that run faster than ur dear six-legged Seabra Sienna," she says. She coughs roughly. My Rorena is exhausted. I wish to protect her from all enemies, including herself.

I say, "I understand the plans, my Queen. We are to meet with this dirt worm of a man called Emperor Thaddeus. I must say again of my deepest objections to my Queen bowing her head to this man of invisible lords and kings living where humans cannot understand."

She tries to hide her amber eyes-rolling. Her assessment of this Emperor Thaddeus falls as low as worms of Doragon's dung heaps. We laugh. For a pleasant moment, we are back in

City Lure, Vanguard's Castle, enjoying dinner and spring wine, the crackling sound and hearty scent of the massive fire pit filled with Wild Tasselwood, knowing that protective Dragons circle above, keeping Doragon safe. Yes, maybe I am in the wrong place and time.

Rorena gently takes my hand. "Come, my Dragon Warrior Knight in dull Doragon leathers, let us go meet this fat little man and bring a feeling of peace so we may win a war. For now, please enjoy the starry ride and all the glitter and ceremony. Many Earth women will wish to eye my handsome Knight, but you are mine forever."

She is always so correct.

The ride to the surface is very beautiful, as always. With her hand in mine, my other on my sword hilt as Knights do, we step onto a new world once again. If my mother and father could see what I saw, they would certainly cover their eyes.

11

Stone
Divisional CMMF (Anastasi) Command
City New Roma
World Empire Sanctuary

By 1400 I am out the motel door getting an air-taxi to the first stop, CMMS Divisional HQ, St. Patrick's Parish. Turns out this station is the only station tasked with security for the big meeting of the Imperium and Emperor. That surprised me. Whoever arranged this job has wide-sweeping power. It is like Queen what's her name has about as much importance as some bureaucrat from a distant world that no one really gives a shit over. I bet the Emperor isn't here. More like on one of his get-away lush private moons. Fat ass should be getting the bullet.

Saska provided civilian clothing. Dressy cheap pants, a dull gray dress shirt, soft-soled shoes, and an ugly-ass tweed sports jacket. Is this what normal people wear? Then there is this sad hologram picture of me dressed in these civilian clothes no way this Italian would ever wear. Fitting for a middle-aged Anastasi lifer. I do like my styles, and this isn't one of them. If I die in this, I deserve any sort of hell available. Oh shit, she included a well-worn copy of bible number 2, as if the first one wasn't upsetting.

I have the credentials Saska left me, proving who I am and why I am there. No idea how deep these go, so trusting she made them sniff-proof. She better have new ones after the job, as in right away. I'm thinking I am not all that good at sneaking around doing this kind of kill work. Good thing this is the last. It's like I woke up and got a job that ends with retirement. End of the story for Stone.

The front desk is womaned by a short scary woman, so short I have to look over and down the counter, who looks up and says, "This better be important. I was about to take my break." I bet her attitude is like the rest of the divisions toward dedication to anyone other than themselves. Never liked poorly trained paramilitary police.

"Prime Sergeant Williams. Been sent here to replace some fella," I say, passing her my credentials. Before I can say another word, she storms off in a huff. People in various uniforms move around, and everyone acts like it's another day at the asshole farm.

A proper uniformed Captain steps up, full parade dress with all the stars and medals. He says, "Praise the Christ. Prime Sergeant, about fooking time. Come with me." I am getting looks. Damn, forgot to salute. Well, better now than end up on a report somewhere. I don't want to screw this clean identity before it's time.

He walks me to the lockers. He says, "Prime Sergeant, you're in charge of this squad of reprobates, replacing the previous Sergeant that just up and got himself killed. You definitely look like a real soldier, not like the dearly departed fat ass you replaced. Poor bastard fell off a ladder at home and broke his neck. His soul may be looking down from heaven, so do a good job, Prime Sergeant."

Yeah, I'm thinking no way the fat-ass sergeant's ladder fall was an accident. The fella's Ident I am using contributed his life, so that's two kills, and I didn't have to do anything. Good deal so far.

The sarcastic Captain goes on, "None of the four under your tender care are worth spit in a fight. It's all about looks and mirrors. You will use a standard four-point enclosure as per Imperium's request, with you following up, like a backup. Why, I have no idea. This entire production is crap. Only you have the authorization to carry a weapon as per orders from far above. The Imperium people have the close in duty but no weapons, nor do our people, except you, Prime Sergeant, but the Imperium people do not know that. Got to keep the pagans thinking we do care about all their requests. They have cleared the entire area of nonessential persons, civilian or otherwise. There'll be squads of Praetorian hiding in shadows. If you see anything bad happening, you are to shoot first, ask questions later. Just be careful the stuck-up Praetorians don't shoot you. I cannot make this any simpler, Prime Sergeant; whatever your name is, just look important, do not make eye contact, and do not screw up by shooting anyone important. Before I forget, there will not be any newsheads anywhere near unless someone gets a whiff and shows up."

"Yes, sir," I say, like a good little Church boy.

"Where do you come from, anyway? Never heard of you."

"Of course, you haven't. I am the real deal. Do not worry; your pension is safe, Captain. Nothing will go wrong, and if it does, I know what to do only if I need to."

He looks like I just poured white paint over him. He grunts and points at the four stupid-looking fools in the now-empty locker room. "Try not to kill any of them."

"Gentlemen," I say pleasantly. They blink like it's morning time. "We have two hours before we have to get on site. Let's pretend we are professionally trained and ready to die. Get this done, the drinks are on me." More blinks with smiles of go fook yourself, Prime Sergeant. Seen that before. No way I do this looking like an idiot in front of quests, pagans, or whatever.

We are all dressed in proper parade uniforms two hours later, looking all so official. My locker had the right uniform, with serious shiny black shoes, worthless in a fight, smart looking cap, and lots of ribbons with the traditional four yellow-white trimmed Sergeant's stripes with the star of David above, making me a Prime. Almost an officer but never one, even in a secret mission. I have to admit, we don't look all that bad and believable. No one will suspect anything but ceremonial presence. None of them have a weapon, although I think one has a sipping bottle. Good for him. These idols don't belong here. Whoever assigned them comes from a way up the food chain. Makes me wonder how many are involved and how deep it goes. Naw, not a fook given.

Under my jacket, neatly tucked, 440 sleeps, a magazine of armor-piercing shells inserted, just in case my target has the worry to wear armor. I could go full bore and risk the ordinance slicing through flesh and bone out the backside. Basically, drilling a hole that some could survive. The squad knows I am armed. They will want to live, so I don't expect any heroic acts.

"One last review," I say to sets of rolling eyes. "The delegation of the Queen, a lady in waiting, a personal aid, a councilor called Theran, four of her personal guards also unarmed, and her husband or whatever they call that relationship."

One of the squad speaks up. "I heard the husband is like old Earth's medieval knight. Rides around on horses. Six-legged ones. Wears useless leather for armor, and get this; he has a sword in a ceremonial sheath. Do not be fooled; it is real, news rumor has it."

We all have a chuckle at that. Yeah, leather armor. Pull out that sword and see what happens.

The guy is full of news. He goes on, "The lot of them are in a baby spaceship. Supposed to be super-fast with a human brain or something. And get this, no, not one support ship. Are they stupid or what? Came here unarmed. Not human smart if you ask me."

"Okay, enough gossip. The Ambassador will be nearby but is not expected to escort the delegation. He will be with the Emperor's entourage, waiting for the Imperium to enter the receiving area. One other will join the dedication, and that is a woman named Eden McGuinness. She is a counselor for the Imperium. No one important. If anything goes upside-down, hit the deck. Do not get in the way of the Imperium people. Well-armed Emperor's Praetorians are lurking like little dogs nearby. They will shoot you and me if we get in the way. This is all about show and gloss." I say all that like I am really in charge. If they only knew. I'm thinking honestly, this should have been a time for the Emperor to show off some shiny muscle with like a marching band and dancing girls.

The gossip guy goes to talk more rubbish. "Shut it down," I snap like a Sergeant would. "Let's get on the job and look pretty."

Not that I never disliked bossing men around, it just got boring being blamed for stupid people. These guys are stupid people.

We get comms word the shuttle from orbit is on its way to the spaceport. It will take about forty minutes for them to disembark and travel to The Christ's Center of Sacrifice. I never have any so-called butterflies. Today I do. Good reason, I guess. I screw up, and I die for certain. I succeed, then it's a new life for me. Maybe this is the weird feeling I've had, like when at the end of a movie Dad and I watched one time. The hero died because he sacrificed for a stupid cause. At least, I thought it stupid cause.

If Dad were here, he'd probably say something like, "Make me proud," or "Break a leg," or my favorite, "Go down shooting." How about I just make you proud for once?

Some people far above Agent Saska have put their lives

and their families on the line to engineer all this backdrop. I will get close. Very close. And no one will think anything different until it's too late. No one will think a second thought. I remind myself this isn't the usual thing SAF did, at least not me, so I better be focused. We had more adequately trained personnel for these missions, but hey, time to expand my resume.

Hell, how hard can this be?

That question is about the same as what can go wrong.

12

Knight Rogan
The Christ's Center of Sacrifice
City Roma
World Sanctuary

WE ARRIVE WITH LITTLE FANFARE BY MEANS OF THESE STRANGE horses called cars. Certainly, plush and comfortable, nothing like a rough-riding warhorse. Take our Doragon creature Seabra. Intelligent and, when bonded, become friends for life. Even so, can a machine such as these travel as fast as a Seabra? My friend Sienna would have some whinnying over this.

The meeting location is an impressive castle, as our Doragonian tongue interprets the Earth word building. Tall to scratch the dull clouds above. Made from materials I care little to understand. For me, I am just a simple Knight dedicated to the service of my Queen, who sits beside me, trying to hide her worry. Nothing will happen to her while I am guarding. Her worry is for an alliance with these deceptive Earth humans.

All my days as a child and then as a soldier in the

Northern Wars, then indentured as an Armsman like my father, I wanted to be a Knight. Now here I am. Nothing more than a symbol of what once was. Am I really to be the last Knight?

Ambassador McGuinness meets us as we arrive at a back door entrance where a few people stand with signs in hands shouting words I rather not understand. How these people discovered our arrival worries me.

The Daystar they call the sun above is warm, and they say it is not raining for once. The aged Ambassador does have a warm, inviting smile—such an example of loyalty. His strong hand pumps mine for a half minute. My mind is cluttered with so many concerns and so many questions. If I could get the wise Ambassador aside, perhaps he could tell me more of the secret man Earth died for.

A set of arms circle me from behind as if I were a captured barbarian. I know those arms. "And here she is, my adopted sister. Eden, I am delighted to see you again." She is squeezing hard. I can feel her powers have grown. With a swift move, I pull her around to envelope her slender frame into a barbarian hug. I get a fleeting struggle with a giggling grunt. She is a wonderful sister I never had.

I wish she could hear my heart's love for her as my sister. Perhaps, she has learned to do such things. If so, my sister, listen to the energy. Today it sings like love birds on Doragon.

"Rogan, I have missed you. Listen, after all this bull is over, you and I can practice arrows like before?"

"Yes, please. Only if you allow me to win." She laughs that sneaky chuckle. I must tell her she is doing as well as any of my soldiers on Doragon achieved in many more years of practice.

Rorena pulls Eden away to allow a bear hug from Ambassador McGuinness. He whispers in my ear, "I will say, my son, you look like a true Knight." He slaps my back hard, then realizes under traditional Doragon clothing, I wear protection as Theran and Rorena demanded. Eden hugs her father fiercely. Rorena tells me the two have had a difficult time over a terrible past relationship.

Eden lets him go. For now, she says.

The Ambassador says to me with a stern fatherly tone, "Relax, Rogan, and observe these pompous proceedings. It's mostly all about show at first. We'll get to the meat tomorrow. Tonight, my friend, we shall drink and sing songs of Doragon. I have taken the time to learn many. I have to run ahead and check on arrangements with the Emperor's delegation. I leave our Queen in your diligent care." He goes ahead but first respectfully head bowing to the Queen. Something I am sure is irritating the Earth humans. It seems none are to bow to another, other than the mere man named Neo they call Emperor. Like a King, they say.

Theran is, as always, standing still, hands hidden inside those long sleeves of that worn battle coat I gave him so long ago, his dark eyes scanning, always looking for any who dare threaten our Queen. I know it is true; Theran would not hesitate to defend the Imperium and Queen, even forfeit his life. I should have trusted him sooner.

Groups of Earth humans are near, clicking devices that produce images of things to share with many who wish to know if we look like humans. Yes, Earth humans, we look just like all of you. We bleed bright red, just like you. Yes, we hug and love just like you.

Lord Theran signals for us to proceed to the meeting room in this huge structure that is so much larger than Castel Lure was. I have never become lost or felt out of place in the vast forests and lands of Doragon. Today, this Armsman become Knight would rather sever my sword arm before retreating outside this building.

Our Royal Imperium Guardsman, well trained in hand to hand to protect the Queen, surround us. Each one has a short blade carefully concealed inside the sleeves of their multicolored tunics. I know for certain all of them will die without thought to protect Rorena.

I notice four other men dressed in flashy uniforms, all looking away as if they don't like us. They circle us. Again, I am dismayed that we, the Queen's own, cannot carry weapons of any kind. Yet, I have my sword, the sword my father-in-law gave me to protect his daughter, my mate, and my Queen. These Earth humans have no idea how well this sword in my hand can summon death to dispatch them to the afterlife they naively believe waits.

None of these Earth humans understand who my Queen is. They think we are nothing more than lesser, sub-human, nothing more than creatures to be pitied. Their minds and hearts are as cloudy as Southern Doragon once was. They cannot see or hear her powers. They cannot see the revealing light of my Queen's presence. They are lost in search of what does not exist, of a creator who looks down from space. I have been in space. There is nothing there but empty hope.

A fifth man is trailing us. He is dressed the same as the uniformed men yet has large yellow markings on his arms. He is always looking around, speaking into mysterious devices. He must be in command over these specially trained men in protection. The man looks at me. His eyes are so green I think of Doragon. He seems like a good man with a pleasant smile, unlike the others who obviously despise our presence.

Lord Theran nods to me. Is there a faint smile on that thousand-year-old face? If Theran is happy, then why should I worry?

I cannot help but feel useless.

13

WE ARRIVE JUST IN TIME TO GET READY. THIS COMPLEX IS THE largest in the Empire, used for anything important Emperor Thaddeus wants to do, like huge sermons right down to meeting with aliens like this Imperium bunch. Dad and I watched so-called alien movies, and these people look like us. No funny-shaped bodies, bulging eyes, skinny parts, and some swampy green color. Oh, and fat heads. They are just like us.

Attached is a hotel for big shots, meeting spaces, and a casino where all profits are for the Church, and no bars, officially speaking. Not my kind of place to party. Good location for our introverted paranoid Emperor Thaddeus, the only direct representative of the Christ to feel safe. Why the Christ can't keep him safe is beyond me.

The plan calls for our honor guard to escort the delegation from the back delivery secure landing to the second-level meeting room, the largest one in the complex. Some not-so-important official of the Emperor meets them at the doorway with condescending babble. I didn't think we could show these guests any more disrespect.

We move down one long hallway with few access doors and plenty of light. Not that I am trained in this, but it seems to me a narrow hallway that can accommodate maybe five people abreast with limited recourse is like a pass between two mountains. Choke point. Downside for me, I have limited choices to get away. Meh, I'll shoot my way out. Must admit I do look good in a pressed shiny uniform with Prime Sergeant stripes.

If they only knew who I am, the irony. Some young woman in a casual uniform but not UWE issue; it has that silly Imperium emblem of a dragon's head gives me a look over. Ah, that's that Eden woman. She is actually an Earth human but not born on Earth. Bah, fake human and a traitor. She greets the Queen, who no one could possibly miss, with a proper bow. I am not bowing.

There is a seriously tall old ass looking man that should be dead by his looks called Theran. Scary fella. Face as white as a snowstorm on old Earth. Bald, big-nosed, and hiding hands inside his sleeves. They say he's like a thousand years old. Hope I don't look that crusty at that age. I'll stay away from him.

It's fooking tense standing here waiting while they pat each other and exchange recipes for space cake. Can't help peeking at the young girl. She's definitely old enough. She thinks I can't see her give me the hey, handsome look. Maybe I could convince her to come back to the good side, charming man that I am. Naw, it's too obvious. I don't give a fook about politics.

Up one level of stairs, then finally off down a long narrow hallway. My squad takes four-point security with me tagging along. The outer ring with their unarmed security all dressed in parade getups. In the center is the core, where the Queen and her people walk. Far too narrow, but it's working fine. It's going to be like shooting fish in a small bucket.

Seriously, these Imperium are a flashy bunch. Look at her, that Queen, all dressed in pompous garb that royalty dropped hundred years ago. She even has a servant caring for the long-ass cape. I can't say she is ugly from what I can see. Maybe all of 5 feet and a few inches tall. Damn, fine-looking face and that long amber hair. Love to run my fingers through while looking into those amber eyes. She looked at me. Right through me. Wow, goosebumps. Can't say I felt comfortable looking back. It's like she recognized me from somewhere. I won't get a chance to watch those eyes go dark. I've watched many eyes go dull with death. This feels different. More butterflies. Ugh.

They said no weapons on their people. They don't realize we know they have long-bladed knives and daggers hidden up those frilly sleeves. Passive scanners reveal all weapons made with just about any solid materials not built with anti-scanner tech. That won't help them at all. UWE weapons rule. 440 is under my tunic, loose, and ready to work.

And there is that fella in the oddest get-up. Looks like something out of medieval times. Wonder if he fought dragons. The news nets say on their world called Doragon, creatures that spewed fire, something like dragons from Earth stories. Every princess's dream. Sounds like little girl stories to me. He looks pretty much out of place. Has a sword strapped to his side and a hand on the top part. Newsheads just love this guy. They say he's handsome. Meh, he's not Italian, so who cares. He's got one hand on the sword hilt. I am pretty sure swords can't stop bullets. Keeps looking at the Queen with puppy dog eyes. They say he is some sort of general who sucks at war. Too bad for you, fella. You're going to be a bachelor again in a few minutes. Nothing personal. I just want to get right with the universe and maybe be an unsung hero who snuck up to put down a pagan Queen. Not that I care about politics or religion. Just here to do a job to save my ass.

Saska said there would be a disturbance. It better happen soon; we are almost to the big doors to the reception room. Then it's up to me. In and out. Escape path back the way we came in. No one will stop me, thanks to this uniform and me making it look like I'm in charge. Saska better be where she said before this fake gets challenged.

The end of the hallway coming up. Two wide doors are open, with a well-lit room behind. Staff dressed in white and gold trim with sparkling smiles start ushering everyone inside. It's now or never, people. If Queeny gets into the large room, it gets impossible to corner her. Time to close range from behind.

The chatter stops dead. Everyone stops moving except for me. I almost can't believe my eyes. Someone in a dragon suit, like kids would have at a scary party, comes out from the open room, knocks one of the white-clad servants over then starts acting like an animal. The dragon roar is bone-chillingly real, at least. I think that's what a dragon would sound like.

440 out to my side. A soft pulse says she's ready. No one is noticing me. All eyes are on the commotion. Game time.

14

Knight Rogan
The Christs Center of Sacrifice
City New Roma
World Sanctuary

I MUST SPEAK TO LORD THERAN AND AMBASSADOR MCGUINNESS after these meetings have been completed about how well organized this day has progressed according to plans. Not pleased about a narrow hallway of perhaps two warhorses' nose to end and mysterious doors without handles to open. I was told men with Earth weapons stand ready to appear, if need be, I suspect from behind those mysterious doors with no markings. As long as we move along quickly, I shall soon relax. I will naturally complain again regarding the no weapons ruling to make my words heard. My hand sits on my sword, where it should be in the presence of Queen Princess Rorena. Some may think the sword is nothing but ceremonial. They could not be more misguided. It is as lethal as a barbarian's ax, quite able to remove limbs and heads in my trained hands. My heart wishes no trouble. Yet, I find myself like a bird of prey waiting, daring a fool to attack so my love will see a Knight and Armsman of Doragon can defend his Queen. Then even the Admirals and Generals and all the council of our Imperium will know I am a man due respect a Knight of the Imperium rightfully deserves.

Why do I feel this sinking feeling? Like when my long-lost friend King Henry and I fought side by side when we fell behind Barbarian lines. Unable to see our hands in the starless, moonless fog-cursed north glass lands. Despite that, the moldy wetness, the fatigue from battle, hunger, and thirst, and many wounds, I felt the same feeling. Something lurked in the darkness. I cannot fail, my love, my Queen. I must be ready for anything to prove my worth for once. Then and only then can I have respect for myself.

The commotion ahead is loud. My hand gently tugs my sword handle, unlocking it from its sheath. I am ready. I am Doragon, the last Knight of my kind.

What is this? A poor imitation of a dragon made for children's delight. Dragons do not make a foolish sound as that. This is not correct. Not planned. I must stop this insult.

I glance at Rorena. She is not frightened. She appears delighted. She looks at me, noticing my concern. I say in a close whisper, "Stand here, be beautiful, while I approach the foolish attempt at a dragon. They have no idea what a real dragon is, do they?" I don't wait for an answer.

The so-called dragon approaches until my hand brings the mocking thing to a stop. "In the name of my Queen, hold there," I say in my best commanding voice. Finally, feeling useful, at least a little.

Looking over my shoulder to see my Queen in hopes she cheers her Knight. Our guards and the other uniformed men circle my Queen. Good. A wall of protection. Excellent.

My eyes must be deceiving me. Between pressing bodies, I see a moving hand with an Earth weapon. The man with yellow arm strips has a hand weapon. I have only seconds. My feet are winged. My sword slides from its home with the sound of a dragon hiss. My leap is like a dragon on prey. I am the last Knight of Doragon.

I am coming, my love.

The tactical world flows as it always does in a battle for me. I see what is happening, anticipate danger, then move quickly. A man's focused mind can sense an enemy sword, an arrow in flight, and a barbarian swinging an ax if he is trained to listen. Many times, in battles, my senses have saved men's lives. Where I stand today, no one uses our weapons. Yet, I can hear the assassin's finger move to trigger a hand weapon to release its metal arrows. I cannot stop the assassin. I can protect my Queen before the metal arrows reach her.

I reach my hand to my love's shoulder, pulling her away, turning my body into a Doragon shield. The special protection Theran insisted on me wearing will stop the metal arrows. I am the shield of Doragon. I am the last Knight.

I see her face. For an instant, I see fear. Then calmness. She knows I will protect her as I always have.

Pain explodes inside my chest.

15

Queen Princess Rorena
The Christs Center of Sacrifice
City Roma
World Sanctuary

WHAT A WONDERFUL SURPRISE I SEE. A MAKE-BELIEVE DRAGON to greet me. Someone thoughtfully reached out to understand Doragon culture and the history of our allies, the Dragons of Doragon. I shall thank Emperor Thaddeus plenty and ask him to bring the person responsible for me to thank personally. Soon, Earth humans will understand we Imperium are just as they are human. These people, these Earth humans, do not know the wonders of our universe, that some creatures are intelligent and some more powerful than flesh and bones. Just as I have, they, too, will discover there are humans every-where and, much to insult their pride, that no one branch is the center of any galaxy.

Now listen to that silly attempt at a roar. I am pleased and amused. If Tarragon were here to see and hear this, he would show them all a true dragon roar, complete with star-hot fire and black belly smoke. This day is going so well. Perhaps my intuition is off from Eden's gloomy presence. I must ask her to guard her thoughts of unnecessary worry so as not to cloud mine. She and Rogan sometimes tire me by nannying me. We cannot fully trust these Earth humans just yet. I do understand this fact. I am positive that none ruling these worlds of Emperor Thaddeus would dare endanger the Imperium Queen Princess while here on this beautiful world. We are fewer than these humans, yet we excel in ways of space and war.

Today will go well for my Imperium. A glorious day I am sure. I will mark this day with flags and celebrations across all my Imperium worlds.

"Rogan, what are you doing?" I say. His hand squeezes my shoulder hard, abruptly swirling me around to face his fearsome anger. I can hear his manly heart pounding. Darkness clouds my vision. Something is wrong, and I foolishly missed it. It is unthinkable. Hate has found me. Oh, please, no, let this day not be the day.

Everything is spinning. A ghostly hand pushes me down. I'm falling. I say into Eden's mind, "Eden, I need you here. The Fathers attack. We are in danger."

All I can hear is nothingness. A heavy body falls on me, holding me still to the floor. I cannot breathe.

"Rogan, is that you? Please let me rise," I gasp. Blackness is overcoming. I need to breathe. I hear his voice grunt. It is him, my Knight protecting me. Has he brought his heavy shield? The time is not now. Please, not now. With what breath I have, I scream, "No." It is as thunder to the ears of the unaware.

Eden appears at the distant edge of conscience. She looks down into my eyes. I feel her power flood my mind.

She is pulling Rogan off. Something is wrong with him. Eden yells, "Medic."

"I am not hurt, sister," I say. Her face is white. "I can breathe now. We must get away from this place. Gather Rogan and the others. Something is wrong, Eden. My heart feels pain, but it's not mine."

Eden says, her words filled with fear. "Rom is injured."

The anger I have never felt before. I push its ugliness away. Not this day. It cannot be today. Please, not today.

Rom lies still nearby. People are doing things to him. "Give me room," I command. People scatter at my thunder voice.

My love's face is dimming into gray. Blood fills the corners of purple lips. Breathing harsh, short gasps. I can hear blood filling his lungs. He is grasping with his sword hand, looking for my father's sword. "Rogan, my love, lay still. Help is coming for you. Focus on my voice. I can help you. Focus on my voice."

His beautiful eyes flutter open. I say, carefully stroking away curly blond hair, "I see you, my love. You cannot hide from me. You will be alright. Focus on me. Hold on to my words as limbs of Doragon's finest trees. Just as we hide from fearsome Tarragon, hide with me now. I will protect you as you protected me."

A man dressed in special white clothing with red crosses reaches a hand under my man. The hand returns, covered in bright red blood. Another hand is hovering over a beeping device. The man's face tells me the worst.

Rom smiles ever so lightly. He harshly whispers, "Are you safe?"

"Yes. There are so many protecting you and me right now that even Tarragon could not approach. Rogan, you must listen to me. You are injured. Please focus on me so I may give you my strength."

Rom moans. "It isn't hurting. I am fine."

"Rogan, hush. Focus on my eyes. Stay with me." I am

begging now. His heart is weakening. Blood runs like a river from the wound.

The man in white softly touches my arm. He speaks, cutting sad words. "I am sorry, miss. The bullets passed through the body armor into the man's chest—explosive armor-piercing shells. Very effective," he says, then looks away, "there is nothing we can do. Too much internal damage. His heart and lungs are shredded. I can give him something to make him comfortable." I nod no.

"Stay with me," my love sputters.

"I will never leave you, Rogan."

My eyes, oh my eyes, do not allow grief to show. I am the Queen; I must not fall.

Rom reaches a bloody hand to catch a tear slipping from my Princess's adoring eyes just as this man bravely did while dragon fire lit the sky above. So many years ago, the memory was as yesterday. Did he know that day he won my heart forever?

I draw his sword, placing it with care into his hand. He sighs as his hand finds comfort in holding the sword he fought battles on our home world of Doragon.

He struggles in the last battle, "Princess Rorena, do not grieve for me," he stops to gather strength. His other hand takes mine, still strong and safe. "I loved you since finding you in the forest. Do you remember?"

I nod. My tears fall on his handsome face.

"I am your Knight?" He asks. "I am your last?"

"Always mine." My mind sees Doragon of old open her arms for one more, the last, to lay at rest. "There is no more, my love. Just you."

I must let go. I must be brave. I am afraid. The time has come.

"Eden?" I scream. "Eden?"

"I am here, sister," she says. Her face is a foul red. Her nose bleeds. She spent all her energy to try and stop death from taking my love from us. I know the path ahead. I must allow this day to occur. I must not interfere.

Rom coughs away dark blood. He weakly smiles. "I am not afraid. My life for yours. My father will be proud of me. Do not be afraid."

I smile. I nod. I allow the day to occur just as it must. I stay my power for the battles to come. My heart is breaking open, pouring love on this man of men. "Take him into your arms, oh Doragon, oh Doragon. Carry my Knight away into the arms of Love, Oh Doragon. Oh, Doragon." I softly sing.

Those so handsome, kind manly eyes slowly give into the grip of death, the light of life ebbing away with each beat of my heart. A breath expels just as the life spirit of my man, my love, my Knight, leaves this time and space.

My heart stops. I will never let it beat again. A sacrifice for all by a true man of one.

Silence envelopes. No one is daring to speak. Eden is crying as I have never heard before from her heart this hateful day.

Lord Theran helps me to my feet. Looking down, I see the lifeless body of the man I loved. He is finally fulfilled.

Anger the likes I have not felt since the Fathers destroyed my home world Doragon threatens to unleash a dragon's fury. With my last ounce of determination, the anger recedes to dark places to keep for another day of revenge. Revenge I shall have. I feel Eden's shivering hand take mine. We share Rogan's blood in our touch.

More people are here. Someone is asking Lord Theran what to do with Rogan. He looks to me for guidance. I say, "Bring him home." Lord Theran solemnly nods.

Eden is beside me; her hands carry Rogan's sword. It is heavy even for her.

People lead us away to another flying carriage. Then in a whirlwind, we are in space. I am empty, yet I feel hope to creep in like a scared rabbit. Come to my lap, scared one. Our future is here.

My mind clears. The day I most feared has come. My enemy thinks I will fall. They think victory is theirs. They believe the last Knight will bring my Kingdom to its end. They are wrong. They have underestimated. Even in his death, I gain strength. They have no idea of what this Queen Princess will do to protect her own, what sacrifices I shall endure.

Behind the many doors of my mind that lead to unknown paths, I hear those hideous ancient men of Hate call my name just as evil taunts. The Fathers wish to say something. I allow the voices to speak as one. The one voice says, "Come for us."

"Be in fear, you hateful men. My Armsman approaches," I say back.

From a Knights End, a new Armsman will rise.

16

Stone
The Christs Center of Sacrifice
City Roma
World Sanctuary

HOLY FOOK, THAT MAN IN HIS SILLY OUTFIT CAN MOVE FAST. HE yells something. Need to act now.

Aiming is not 100 percent clear, but it can't miss. I never miss. 440 whispers. Got two off. Armor tipped and explosive on entry. Intelligent ammo always wins.

All hell is breaking loose. Time to move.

Someone grabs my gun arm. One of their guards. Bad idea. Jabbing a finger deep into an eye breaks my arm free. 440 back under jacket. One of my guys tackles the screaming missing eye fella. Then it's on. Our guards are on their guards. Perfect chaos. For good measure, I kick a couple of people, no idea who they are.

I didn't see the impact. People are screaming something about she's down. Good. Job done. I never miss. Got to get out of here before that fool with the sword tries to stab me.

That tall dead looking guy is coming for me. Not today, Mr. Greedy Death.

"Going for help," I yell, in hopes of causing more confusion. Well-armed, fully dressed military, not uniformed Anastasi or the Praetorian Guards as promised, are pouring in from the hallway's doors. They ignore me. Emperor's personal guards, specially trained as well as SAF. They go nuts whacking anyone that isn't laying still.

Finding the back door to the alleyway. More military. Big deal. Dad told me once about an expression called Keystone cops falling over themselves. This is it.

Air cars everywhere above. Armed. Copters and drones too. Sirens going off all over now. And I just walk away like I am going for dinner and a movie.

Must give Saska a big kiss when I see her.

17

Queen Princess Rorena
Aboard Adona
Unknowable Location

WE ARE ABOARD OUR STARSHIP ADONA. LORD THERAN IS WITH us. The man is a giant of support, taking care of all the matters needing attention. In the cold cargo container, under the belly of Adona, wrapped in commoners' rags, lies the body of Knight Rogan, my man and lover. We are bringing his body home to New Doragon, where we shall mourn for as long as I wish.

Eden lays Rogan's sword at my feet as our custom for a fallen hero. She cannot console herself. Placing a royal hand, not a sister's hand, on her lowered head, I say, "Quiet your heart. We require your dedication to move forward. We have a Kingdom, a union of peoples to rule. They will need our calm words, or we risk igniting our people to demand a war with Emperor Thaddeus we cannot afford. Our Imperium needs calm. I need my closest counselors to stand by my side. Do I have this from you, Princess Eden?" I use her royal title to emphasize my wishes.

She takes a deep breath, wipes away tears then deeply bows in a rare showing of respect. "I serve at the pleasure of my Queen."

Lord Theran speaks up from his conversation with Adona. "I, too, my Queen, am at your service."

"We are pleased," I say in the royal voice. "Lord Theran, tend to all arrangements required to transport Our fallen Knight to rest. Any of Our fallen on this dreadful day do the same."

To Adona, our marvelous starship with the mind of a human and the power of mysterious technology, I say, "Adona, please make way to our home as quickly as possible in a manner that none will know. Also, please inform Our battleships, Vanguard and Gunnar, to reappear from invisibility and then move to position themselves at a safe but imposing distance from the world below for a period of no more than one Earth standard day. We wish to give this treacherous Emperor Thaddeus of the United World Empire something to focus on his fears instead of the imaginary forces of a red-horned devil. Instruct the commanders of each ship not to engage unless it becomes impossible to ignore. Once the time expires, they are to make all haste back to our space. We must prepare for any eventuality."

Adona says, her voice always calm, but I can detect a hint of proto-human sorrow in those simulated thoughts, "As you wish, Queen Princess Rorena. We will arrive at World New Doragon within one day." I feel our presence slip into a universe no one truly understands as the stars around us disappear into nothingness.

I sit in a seat, the one Rogan enjoyed the most, where he could see out one of the few true windows. As much as my man complained about space, he did secretly sit in wonder at all the mysteries even though I had no understanding. Eden comes to sit at my feet as she does when we speak openly.

"Speak your mind, sister Eden. I can feel the anger in your heart."

"How can...how can you be so calm? I want to kill the man that did this. Rogan is...was my brother."

I say back with the calmness of a Queen, not of a grieving lover, "No, sister, this killer of our Rogan will suffer at my pleasure. When he is located and still alive, we must preserve his life. A dead man cannot experience royal justice. He will live to regret this day. He will never know love as I have. I shall dangle love as the most tempting fruit, then snatch it away before the foul mouth tastes. He will come to know the true pain of lost love. I will invade his dreams with an army of dragons breathing fire to burn his heart from within." She has not grasped the connection between Rogan's assassin and the man Admiral Edison, at great Imperium cost, ensured escape from dying Earth is the same man who this day ended Knights forever. Convincing her to stand down for the greater love will take much patience.

Eden says, "Forgive me, sis, I got to clean up." I see she has blood, my Knights blood, on her clothing. "Please, as you wish, sister," I say.

Once she has retired to clean herself, I say to Lord Theran, "Come, council with your Queen and friend."

He stands taller than any man. His normally emotionless face frowns, something quite rare. I say, "Quiet your heart, my very old friend. We have much to do."

"They will be angry you are still alive," he says, his deep voice struggling with emotions.

"Angry, yes. We shall work that to our advantage. My father always told me angry barbarians always make angry mistakes. Let them stir themselves just as the maidens turned milk into that taste sponge you have come to enjoy. Such anger will help expose who they all are, one by one. We shall enjoy the fruitage of our siring."

He asks the question I fear, "This is the day?"

I solemnly nod.

He says, "A dangerous game we play, my Queen. Your life is all the Imperium has held together since we were forced from our home worlds. The Fathers would be quite joyful in your demise. The Earth's human empire would fall in little time without the Imperium to stop the Father's aggression. We fall, all will fall."

"Your insights are correct. Until we know all the villains, we can do nothing more but remain defensive. Time and Patience, odd cousins of Love, will be our allies."

"Agreed," he says. He pauses. I know why. I wish to tell him all, but to do so would change our path with many stones to stubble our feet.

"My Queen. . .."

"Yes, Lord Theran, I knew the risk was there, waiting. I knew the traitors would move soon. Their slime trail of thoughts is not hidden from me. There are forces at work here hiding in plain sight."

"What of this Emperor Thaddeus? He is a terrible little man fearful of his own shadow."

"Perhaps Emperor Thaddeus should shiver in fear that I still live. Perhaps I should decide to allow the hateful Empire of the Fathers to do as they please. How long will these arrogant Earth Humans last against the hordes of mindless EOF minions? Look at their burned planet Earth."

"I must ask of the Fathers. Do you see their hateful hand in these matters?"

I sigh. My body is begging for rest. "Yes, my old friend. I suspect when all the layers of betrayal peel away; we shall find their skeleton hands dripping with innocent blood. As I have taught you, the Fathers think they walk along a path they choose, yet we know behind them are the strings of Hate."

"I am sorry, my Queen, I must beg. Command me, and I

shall travel to the Father's moon and end this forever," he says, taking to his knees.

"Oh, if it were only true, I would dispatch my Lord Theran to slay those hateful 13. Even with my powerful hand, we cannot defeat them on our own. All in good time, my friend. We must grow Our human weapon that even they cannot overcome. Rise to your feet. I enjoy your comforting shadow. Yes, my friend, this day came upon us unexpectedly. It has occurred. Please tell me of my Ambassador McGuinness. Is he safe?"

"Yes, he went to the Imperium Embassy. He is doing what he does best in his charming way while letting the Emperor and his cronies know we are not to be trifled with. If anyone can cause order from disorder, Allen can do so."

"Excellent. Send Ambassador McGuinness a message. We are pleased. Continue to hint at war with the Imperium until I decide otherwise.

"Now, Eden will soon return. Please keep these words between you and I until I say differently. It is not the time for her to understand the identity of Rogan's murderer."

"As you wish," he says. "I shall be attending matters for a Royal homecoming of our fallen Knight."

I almost want to let the tears flow at Lord Theran's thoughtful caring of my Rogan's body.

Adona moves us through realities disconnected from our physical space. Time is not the same here. In my mind, I see things. Events that occurred and sometimes those that wish to occur. I see the man I foresaw in my dreams, the murderer of my Rogan. I knew the attack would come in time, but for me, not for my Rogan. I see the murderer's heart. I see a hidden love he runs from. One day I shall take that secret love from Rogan's murderer. He can never hide from me. When I have purified him from destructive anger and hate, I shall unleash him upon Hate itself. The murderer will become our weapon.

Eden wakes me. "Sister, I do not know his name as of yet.

Who he is will soon surface. Many will want to kill him." She sounds pleased.

I find a knowing smile to cover my sadness. I say to Eden, "I already know his name. He must not fall into enemy hands. You and Lord Theran do whatever is necessary to secure the man's life. Clear his name and face so that none will recognize him with the help of Adona's powerful methods. That pathetic life will become ours to do with as we please all in due time, but first, he will suffer."

Lord Theran, a man without emotions, looks as though he would rip the moons of Doragon apart to avenge Rogan. "What is the name of this man?" he asks, his voice so strong with energy it rattles into spaces they cannot see.

Eden steps close. Her face is focused on hate. "Yes, sister, tell us the bastard's name."

I cannot tell my friends that the man they hate will become Our Armsman to replace the fallen Knight. I cannot tell them this is the man I have prophesied to battle Hate with hate. In good time all secrets will come into the light of the Daystar.

I speak the murderer's name.

"Stone."

18

Stone
Construction Site
City New Roma
World Sanctuary

"It's done," I say. "Quite full of myself, I must say."

Saska isn't looking happy.

"C'mon, I did the job. Why so glum?" Now I wonder if she knows what's in store for her. I hope not. Makes it much harder.

"Look in the backseat. Get changed before someone spots you. The entire city is in arms. The CMMS is setting up checkpoints everywhere. Even with my clearance, it won't be easy getting you safe. The Emperor has released the planet side Army into local command. Personally, I should just shoot you now and get a nice pay bump."

She is pissed. Not sure why yet. In the back seat, I find new clothes, a stupid sports hat of some baseball team I had never heard of, and big shaded eye goggles. Of all things, a white walking stick.

"What's the white stick for? Are we playing some sort of sexual fantasy? I don't mind, just as long as you're not hitting me with the stick."

"No, it's not for that. You will probably enjoy it. The clothes and white cane, with the glasses, are a disguise. Put those glasses on, and not only do they cover half your smart-ass face, no one can scan anything past them. The bag holds a real-looking wig and facial hair. You are a blind man I was escorting to a Goodwill church function when we got caught up in the lockdown emergency. We agents have our pet projects for helping the community. I'd rather actually go blind, but it's worth the credits upstairs gives for our pretended concern."

"Why are we sitting here in an empty parking lot for ground cars? Should we not be in the air leaving smoke behind?" I say, putting the clothes on as quickly as I can. Stuffing the uniform deep under the seats.

"Not yet," she says. "I got a tip that a military two-person HAR is coming here to investigate why someone is in a closed construction site, that being you and me. About five minutes before you showed up-thanks for taking your fooking time. I got a stand-in place order until they okay me. I knew it could happen. Hence the disguise because your stupid face is probably on the nets by now. So, the story is, your ID in your pocket says your name and civil address. Answer any questions along those lines, and let me do the rest of the talking. Did you dump the 440? Right? Like I told you before."

I smile my answer.

"The Christ in a spaceship, Stone. Fook. Keep it offline and hidden. They sniff that damn gun, we have problems."

"Okay, chill. We knew there would be some lockdown." Not telling her the 440 series I have is very difficult to detect with most standard equipment.

"Some? It is going Empire wide now."

I frown. Did she say Empire wide?

"Hold on, what about the shady Imperium coup? People here should be dancing in the street, right?"

She goes to answer, but the HAR arrives.

"And speak of the devil's own," I say, pointing ahead at the HAR. "Heavy Armored Rover. Got to admit that name has a convincing ring. Two-person armored patrol vehicle, ground only. Minimal armaments. No big deal. It's used for recon, mostly." That gets me a dirty look.

"Stone, stop pointing; you're blind, remember?"

The HAR stops in front of us. Out jumps two fully armored military fellas. At least they took off the face protection. Then it hits me. I ask just as she lowers the side windows and flashes her badge, "Military. Army? Not Anastasi? Did not expect that response. They must be seriously pissed over a dead Queen. She was kind of sexy, though."

Saska mumbles, "Shut up. Be blind."

I want to say, can blind people not talk too?

One army fella, a private, stands on my side out of my reach. The other, a corporal, starts talking to Saska on her side. She is telling a good story. Fortunately, the super dark goggles I am wearing like a blind guy are normal inside, as in I can see just fine. So far, they haven't done any scanning with hand units. Good. As EMF safe 440 is, best to be ready for anything.

The Corporal asks, "Sir, your name and ID, please. Now."

I fumble around, overplaying the part. Almost passed the papers as if I could see. Saska saved that juicy moment. She is right; I can see clear as day from my side of the glasses. Guess the manufacturers didn't worry about preventing brightness for a blind man.

The Corporal says, "Okay, this looks fine. Nice of you to show an interest in the community, Agent. You lucky Agents get some nice perks, like this agency air-car. It's sick looking. How fast can you move in open air?"

I so want to say something like wanna find out, asshole.

Take you and drop you at high speed a few thousand up. Saska says, "Classified." That is a good answer, I think.

"Bad day for the bitch Queen, yes?" The Corporal asks. I think he's a genius. I just killed her. Yeah, bad day and all. According to the intel Saska told me before, certain people should have taken over the Imperium by now. No Queen, no leader. Oh well, maybe the Emperor's response has to look like he cared.

Saska says, "Yes, it is. For all of us in some ways." I can hear the power windows start to sneak up. She's trying to give them a hint to fook off.

"I mean, Agent lady, how can they think threatening war will work? Don't they know who Emperor Thaddeus works for?"

Saska says, "Funny way to put that, Corporal. Yes, I agree, not an optimal situation. If you don't mind, I need to get this man to his destination. Obviously, he can't get anywhere on his own with all this upset. Then my HQ needs my presence with matters I cannot discuss. You understand?"

"Yeah, got you on that one. Hey, how about you and me take a quick look inside my HAR? We have secrets too."

I can hear Saska almost gag. I know what her gags sound like after our time together. This is going to get really interesting.

She says, "Not today, soldier." I hear the window try to go up, but peripheral vision tells me his arm is holding it in place.

"C'mon, I insist. No one will know you took a few minutes to check out what the Empire Army has for weapons. Call it Agency research. No one will know, Agent. I can call the stop in as all good or needs backup."

"Corporal," Saska says, using a tone I haven't heard before. Makes me want to stand at attention. "Get back to your post. We may be at war."

I hear the distinct sound of a handgun coming out of a dry, barely used hip holster. I can't 440 out just yet. Need to kill two really quick from a sitting position inside this cramped space. No way I get 440 out without getting shot first. The private has an I'm-so-happy-grin but has the training to know to keep some distance from my open window. I can't get a lock from where I am on him. The two undersexed assholes picked a good place for a forced encounter with a woman with authority. Gotta keep those women in place, right, you worthless pigs. Some men make even me sick.

As for Saska, she will have her service weapon on her back, where she always carries it. No way she can draw and shoot. It means both of us are in a tight spot.

I wish I could poke what to do into her head. Think Saska. The impossible tactical situation inside the car. Get out. I'm blind. What trouble can I cause? They will ignore me.

She must have read my mind. She says, "Okay, let's have a look. Can we make it quick, you and your happy looking private?"

"Of course. In and out. Trust me on that."

She gets out. The corporal leans in and whispers, "Stay put, blind man. I am authorized to shoot under martial law."

I'm thinking martial law. All-out military presence. Talk of war. Something didn't go as planned with the takeover. Our Empire government should be dancing in the streets.

The two army fellas take sides on Saska as if it's an escort, walking her to the open side door of the HAR. Nothing pleasant for her inside that armor. She is in for a quick and ugly time. I wonder if she will shoot them. Can't let her have the fun.

First, the Corporal's head explodes. Then a half-second later, the Private. And they didn't even get a chance to realize a blind man had just killed them.

Saska turns around. No, not surprised; she's mad.

"I have to say I love those explosive shells."

"Stone," she growls. She looks around for anyone near. "I was going to do that out of sight. You are such an ass."

"Not bad for a blind guy, right? Relax, I had the silencer on. No Sat or Drones will bother with a common stop like this. The two idiots were on their own. I'm betting they called it in as all clear. I know the army. They barely can find their weapons, let alone run security."

As quickly as possible, we put what's left into the HAR. In seconds we are airborne. She pops out her SatCell and calls the agency's control point, informing them she just observed a gunfight between local gangs and an army HAR.

"Good idea," I say.

She just cusses me out. That's fine. I like it. Feeling good now. My future is back on track.

Looking forward to freedom and lots of retirement, whatever that is. "Maybe I should have just hit them with the white stick. Come on. I saved you from two assholes having their way."

"You don't think I could have taken care of them inside a cramped HAR?"

I think for a second about that. "Good point."

"Stone, you really need to shut the fook up. Have you no regrets ever?"

"No," I answer in a snap. "Never have. Gets in the way of work. You should learn how it will help you be all you can be, Agent Saska."

She looks at me, then puts the AirCar on full auto. "We are out of the city, so we can relax some. I'm taking you to a covert house location we don't use anymore, about 60 from the locked-down city. Don't let the trees flying by under the belly trouble you. Avoiding the basic radar systems. This is a covert car anyway, so we have some more protection." She taps her earpiece. "The chatter on the nets says nothing about us. So, we are good for now. No more shooting. Understood?"

"Body count since I started this whole mess is 14. Not bad, right? Can I have a kiss? All this shooting and killing gets me happy?" I add a wink for clarity. Yeah, I am an ass at times. She should be happy I haven't decided to kill her yet.

She looks at me like I asked for the Earth's old moon. Someone already bought it anyway. She says, "Stone, do you have any idea what you did?"

"Yeah. I did the plan. Kill the Queen. People take the throne because, as you said, they are right there waiting in the, what did you call it, the wings. With all the talk of full Military out and martial law, I think the takeover people didn't move right away. So, what? They will sort it out."

"You don't know, do you? How the fook did you miss? How the fook did you, the great SAF-trained killer, not see what you did?"

Now I am pissed. "You're ruining a good day for Stone. I took the target out. Two shots, chest high with the armor-piercing explosive intelligent tips. I stuck 440 in between two bodies, judged the angle and distance as trained, and popped two off. I saw her fall. What the hell is going on?"

Saska rubs her face hard. She looks around like someone else is going to answer. Below, I see the evergreen treetops whizzing by, telling me either she is not lying about a hideaway in the middle of nowhere or she wants to bury me in the woods. My gut tells me I won't be getting any kissing or other thank-you activities later.

"Stone, you fooking fool. We are on a war footing with the Imperium because the Queen is still sitting on her potty throne. You missed her. The people waiting to take over to bring this war forward now cannot risk a move on the throne. I am betting they are already being beheaded. Our Empire is on full alert for war. The Imperium Ambassador is screaming for revenge. Two battleships of the Imperium are sitting over New Roma, waiting for one wrong step."

"Huh?"

"You didn't kill the Queen. You killed her husband."

All I can come up with is, "Oh."

19

Stone
Keepers Forest
World Sanctuary

WE'RE MOVING ALONG AT THE MAXIMUM SPEED THE SOUPED-UP Agency air-car can give. Nothing below us other than trees, hills, more trees, and a few baby lakes. Saska isn't talking yet. That's okay. Spending the time running everything through in my head, trying to figure out what went wrong.

All of a sudden Saska shoots out words, "You missed. Stone. You missed the Queen. You killed her husband. He must have gotten in front of the shot in time. He died right there. They took his body with her and bugged out before anyone here could ask questions. They are probably back in Imperium space with the spaceship she has. Stone, the Imperium, is rattling swords about this, daring us to make a move. You do know they have technology that masks their warships until they decide to drop weapons we never heard existed in all our warlike past.

"Fortunately, the Emperor was not on World Sanctuary. He needed plausible deniability. I bet he's somewhere deep inside a moon. What does that tell you? This whole thing was to topple their government in one quick move, and it failed miserably because of you."

I say something stupid, "I bet the Queen is pissed."

"Stone. God damn it. They are thinking of a two-front war now. The Christ help me."

I think for a moment. I say, "I did the job. Not my fault that fella dressed in a stupid medieval outfit with an even stupider sword managed to get in the way. Last I saw him, he was pushing the costumed dragon away. My timing was perfect."

"Stone, I hate to bash your fragile manhood, but your timing is rarely perfect."

That hurt more than the time I got shot four times.

We arrive at a one-room cabin in the woods. Woods that spell you are nowhere filled with things that want food. Any food. Saska isn't talking much. I think she is worried about the repercussions for the United World Empire. As for me, I am worried about what Don Falcone is going to say. This job was my way out—the last chance. And a glorious way to end a bang-up career. Hanging from a meat hook while some sadistic cheerful master torturer peels skin off slowly, piece by piece, is not where I want to go. I hear they start with the man's most important part. I'll put 440 to my own head first before they touch that very important part.

Saska goes to the cabin door to leave. "Hey, where you going?"

"I must report back. I've been tasked to investigate two dead army personnel with missing brains. If you make a wisecrack about that, so help me, I'll shoot you and leave the body for the animals."

"How long will I stay here? Not the survivalist type. Yeah, I saw the food stocks, water, and a viewer hookup for videos."

"Wait a week, maybe two, then take the ground SUV

vehicle from under the lean-to with full automation for blind shity drivers. Head anywhere but near me. Yes, you and I can never meet again. Leave this world. Identifying as a blind man will help because, believe it or not, there are good people, so stay blind. Notice I included a credit chip. It's not refillable, so don't try."

"I can't fly or drive. If it were a helicopter, that would work."

She shakes her head. "It is automatic mAI made for blind people, you ass. Pay the fook attention."

I think I may miss her whit.

She says, "Figure it out. The bag of stuff has a limited SatCell. No nets and uplinks. Just call someone who cares. I'm gone. Good luck."

I just had to ask. "Wait, for fooks sake. No goodbye kiss?"

She's gone. I have no idea if anyone is going to pay me. Kinda back to where I woke up only to repeat a nightmare over and over.

Here I am in the middle of the woods, without any way to leave. Blind man disguise? Really dumb idea. Blind man car? Wouldn't that just draw attention?

She isn't aware that her life is now safe. Why would I kill her as a loose end if the Queen didn't die and I am not collecting my due? Well, it makes sense to me. So I wave goodbye like a good blind man.

How the hell did I miss Queeny? She is going to be forever on my ass to kill me for this. Hell, what's one more hate stick wanting me dead? No way I say sorry for her stupid husband giving up his life. No way I do that for anyone. No, that's not true. Maybe Selene. She was a good woman.

First thing in my immediate plan. Food. Then hope for some booze here.

The SatCell is the most basic model. The only number I can remember that count is the worst and only friend I have.

"Hey, Jimmy, it's your worst nightmare calling."

"It's about time you called. The Don wants to see you. Where are you?"

"Out on the deck, actually kind of nice, looking up at the puffy clouds and blue bits of sky, while birds and noises I can't identify circle around like a platoon of marksmen. It's nice here. The problem is, I don't know where it is."

"Stone, for a SAF elitist, why can't you understand SatCells? I have your location fixed. Bad idea to have it unlocked. Try not to kill all the wildlife."

"Well, whatever that little gray fluffy-tailed thing is, it's rubbing front paws like a devious criminal about to commit a murder."

He disconnected.

This isn't going to be fun.

I sleep instantly. The dreams are not like usual. I see molten fire and mountains with snow tops. I see that Queen. Her face is calm, but she yells things I can't understand. Stupid and weird things happen. Swords and dragons come and go. Another woman I had never seen before, so old the wrinkles almost cover her face, tells me to wake up. "The nights end," the crackling voice says.

Jimmy is pounding on the door.

20

Stone
Uncle Dev's Heritage Meat and Cheese Shop
City New Caroline
World Caliadne

JIMMY AND I SIT IN A GROUND-TAXI WAITING FOR SOMEONE TO call us inside, where Don Falcone is supposed to meet with me. I insisted on a public place. It wouldn't matter, anyway. This isn't really a public place. Someone in the Don's family owns the joint. Why didn't he pick a bar?

I point and say, "That was a perfectly good blind man's truck from the cabin. Why didn't we take that?"

"Seriously, are you that stupid all the time," Jimmy spits out? "It was most likely tracked, and booby trapped. Boom for you."

He is right; I didn't think of that.

"How much did you drink for the few hours sitting there in that cabin? I can smell your breath. You stink."

I smile weekly. "There was a lot to down. Couldn't leave it for the animals, right? Booze helps me sleep. How long do we wait in this shit taxi without a follow-up drink?" I ask. "Not nervous, just asking."

"The only time you were ever nervous was when your mom took you off the tit. Didn't know where the next suck came from." Jimmy says.

"Seriously, Jimmy, insulting my mother is worthless. I've already decided to kill you. No need for more reasons."

He laughs. "You may not get past this day. Why the Don is even bothering with you is not making sense. Don Falcone doesn't take a dump without finding a way to get money for it. Maybe someone up there likes you. Or maybe down there." Jimmy does the pointing to make sure I understand up and down. Idiot.

Jimmy's SatCell chimes. "Time to go in. Just sit and answer questions. Maybe I can fix this."

Inside the mirror of a 19th-century replica Italian restaurant sits four goons. They look confident about who is in charge. A man dressed like a cook closes and locks the door. All the blinds are drawn. There is a smell of meat cooking. How interesting, it's pork.

"Doesn't this remind everyone of a bad video?" I say as cheerfully as I can. The goons give me an unfriendly look. I nod no. Jimmy says, "Give it, or it's over." There goes 440.

From the kitchen door walks Don Falcone. All full of himself. Looks like he just got off the golf course. He takes up a chair to sit a few feet from me. Jimmy wisely gets distance from me.

"Look at you, the famous, or shall we say infamous, Stone. The man who murdered the wrong target," says Don Falcone. I can smell a mix of manly cologne and booze. He purposely enunciates every word like it had its own razor-sharp edges meant to cut exposed flesh. He is mistaken because I don't care.

At this point, I may as well go all in and piss the top Family leader off more, if that is possible. Judging by the man's obvious red cheeks under a leather-tanned Italian face, I say as if it's a consolation prize, "Someone had to die that day."

The Don is off the chair, throwing anything he can find off tables. Two vases, which looked like real glass and expensive, crash to the floor. He stops to look down at the glass and says, "Pity, they were from Sicily. Old, much expensive."

A slender fella saunters in from the kitchen, about my height but a thinner build, dressed in a tactical black turtleneck and, judging by his adjusting pants, has an ego hanging there. He isn't like the other goons. Something is different in the way he carries himself.

Finally, the Don calms down. "Do you have any idea the trouble you caused?"

"Sir, I can only guess the trouble I caused. You can, if you want, explain." Yeah, I said that. My mother used to slap my mouth for that kind of backtalk. All I get from the Don is a head-shaking groan.

"Okay, Stone, for the slow in the room, here are the details that slip by you. You killed the wrong target. You killed the Imperium Queens' husband. She is about ready to open a war on us. That's you, Stone, me, and the rest of Earth humans. Even I know we cannot win against the Imperium and the other goons. I won't name the others who died, others that will die, that worked to set this up. That included the man you took out in the radiation zone. He talked too much."

Can't let that go. "You mean the evil Empire of the Fathers, right."

The Don's response was instant. "Shut up while I talk. Interrupt me again, and I'll have my men pull your damn tongue out."

I nod, keeping my face as blank as possible. I'm fooked. Everyone knows it. Jimmy knows it. I know it. So what to stick my tongue out?

"Now, the Imperium Queen has gone into hiding. We will

never get another chance. Guess who calls me to whine like the bitch he is?"

A few moments go by. He told me to shut up, so you can't blame me for doing what I'm told, for once.

The Don, always a gentleman, goes to the bar and makes a drink. Expensive rum leftover Earth's stock. A drink makes its way to me through a couple of guards. Guess the Don isn't ready to get too close to me.

"The Emperor himself. His Holiness. The true representative of the Christ on Earth. Well, when there was a Mother Earth, of course. His Holiness tells me how disappointed He is. My presence in His plans for putting the pagan Queen, as He calls her, into a grave on a lifeless moon is ruined. Because of my incompetence," the Don says, his hands swirling around, splashing irreplaceable rum everywhere. "Stone, you were in the military, the SAF, you know shit floats down. It also manages to collect in certain places on the way down. Big brown gobs are collecting on me. Do you understand without a diagram? The entire plan has many faces without names. You, Stone, opened the floodgates."

I am thinking I wish the man would stop with the dumb attempts at coloring pictures like I am dumb and just get to the point.

"My incompetence," he yells. "All you had to do, Stone. Point and shoot. Point and shoot. Queen dies. We all go back to normal. You have no idea what normal is, do you, Stone?"

I'm not answering because my normal has nothing to do with regular normal. That's where I belong, in a world outside of normal people slaved to the Church. SAF is where I was to die in flames. Instead, I gotta be here and deal with this self-satisfied overgrown Italian spoiled ass. What does he know about normal anyway? He's about as evil as Mother would often say that the devil himself would be impressed.

"Are you going to at least explain?"

"Sir, it is, as I explained before. I had a clear line of sight.

She was right there looking at me as if she knew what was going to happen."

The Don interrupts with a stop hand. "Yes, I have heard the stories. She has quite a way with words and presence. Something they say about her eyes. When she looks into your eyes, she can see a man's thoughts. Is this what happened to our man Stone? A little woman from another world mesmerized poor weak SAF Stone. Did she arouse you? Is that all you think about, Stone, drinking, and womanizing? Getting your tongue wet and little pecker cleaned."

I want to say, and that's how different from you? Trying not to reply. Focusing on letting anger grow. Anger is a powerful emotion. Just enough to burn through the walls of a head-banging hangover. The trick is not to let on.

"Don Falcone, it is, was one of those things that happens. No one could figure the man would jump out of nowhere. I swear he was like a wall of a man flying across right between her and me. I should have had time. No one can fly. I don't know how he knew to move. Everyone did their part in getting her in place where I had access. I drew and pulled in less than two seconds, and that's it. He was dead. If not for me using AP rounds, he would have had broken ribs. If he had not worn body armor, maybe one shot would have gotten to her. I fired; he went down. She's looking at me with those eyes. Don Falcone, I have looked into the eyes of many a man and woman before and after I did my job. Whatever they say about her is spooky true."

The room is dead quiet. Can't say I didn't explain what happened, almost resorting to stick pictures for the stupid. The Don looks at his drink, pours more, and downs it with an audible gulp. He walks in his Italian I'm-the-Caesar-strut around the restaurant like I'm prey for a lion. I bet he's never seen a lion. Mother took me to the last zoo on Earth near Tokyo. One of the nice things she did. Of all the times, a memory of her bloated red face laying in the sewer decides to spoil this moment of being crapped on by Don Falcone.

"Do you wish to beg for your life, Stone SAF hero?" the Don says.

"Not a chance, Don Falcone," I say. My head is clearing away the cobwebs. Almost feel my feet again. I always wanted to die in an alcoholic haze. Just not this way by this man's hand.

"How can I let you live? Do you understand the loss the Families must endure because of this? The kind Emperor wills we must increase our tithe to the Church by 10-fold. A righteous penance. I also promised something of yours, Stone. Can you provide a guess to amuse me?"

"Rather not play the game if it's all the same," I say. Clenching my hands to get ready. Identify any weapons and where the exits are. Counted four goons plus the mysterious fella standing all relaxed like by the kitchen door. The rest are non-targets, for now. I'm seriously dehydrated, exhausted, and not in a good mood. Those are not good odds.

"What means shall I dispense with you?"

Lots of glass chunks here and there. A weapon if I can figure out how to get a piece in hand.

"If given a choice, Don Falcone, I like to go down fighting. You know, to the death. Hero-like."

His laugh is from the feet up, filling the small restaurant. "Stone, I knew in my heart this is the man I understand. We are the same on this topic—unfortunately, not my time. Pick one of these men."

"Let me look around," I say, pretending to rub the sleep away. I see a sliver of a broken vase not far away. Suppose I can move fast enough; it's mine. Think I can get to the Don before anyone else. I'll die, but I'll die on my feet.

"Because I am the Don and you are destined for brimstone, I choose one for you," he says like it's a better idea.

"Yes, I do not play fair. How else can a man as I rule the Families without a heavy hand."

"Which one," I ask. Closing eyes, clearing the mind. Just like SAF taught, know where the enemy is. In a field, behind a barrier, hiding, or standing nearby. Know the faults and strengths of one's enemy. Do something the targets won't expect, even if it's obscure, to get them off balance.

The Don pours another drink and takes it over to the mysterious man by the kitchen door. He refuses the drink. Definitely not a normal goon.

"Fook me," I say.

"Yes, Stone, fook you," the mysterious man says, pointing at me.

The Don says, his standard English melting into heavy Italian accent, "Fook you for screwing me. I give you a chance. Look the disrespect you return. Stone meet Lieutenant McCoy. He is an active officer of, well, I can see you have guessed."

"SAF," I say. Looking at the Lieutenant's face, I see an ever-so-small smirk. Gotta wipe that away. "Moonlighting? You're just a baby, not out of training. Think you are all that and then some."

He looks at me like I am meat on a plate. "No one retires. No one leaves the SAF on two feet. Just for the tactical tags, call me Good-looking. Yes, we all know your way of tagging targets. Rather clever, I thought." I'm thinking I want to like him, but again, can't have two smart-asses in the same room.

The Don waves the other guards to back up. "No one interferes. Stone, this is not going to fulfill my revenge. It will be close. Not paid."

"Don't write me off just yet, Don Falcone." I barely get the words out when a fist hits me square jaw side-on. Damn, that kid is fast. The floor feels kind of good. Think I'll stay here for a moment.

While lying there stunned, I say, "You should tag me as

Mr. Better-Than-You-Will-Ever-Be." That pissed him off. Good.

"Get up, old man. At least die with a little dignity," Mr. Good-looking says.

Don Falcone laughs while reclining his feet to a tabletop like he's at a social visit. If I could get to him, this would be all over in many ways.

"How about you try to get me up?" I say. A boot to the ribs gets my attention. "Okay, give me a second."

"I've heard about you, Stone. Disgrace to the SAF. Drunken old fool. You should have been shot and dumped on a dead moon. You know what impressed me? You dared to do the worst thing. You killed one of your own. Yes, I know all about that."

"That isn't very nice, kid," I say—time for me to wind him up. Buy more time. Then the kicks start, so I crawl away, slowly, towards a weapon. Damn, that winded me good. I sputter, "I did an old lady once; she kicked better than that."

"Get up and fight me," Mr. Good-looking says, gritting his teeth like an animal. Anger with purpose and focus is good. Blind anger is not so good.

"Come down here and fight like a man," I say.

He tries for a head kick out of frustration. Caught the foot. Twist the foot. He's too big and balanced for a complete fall. Sweep my leg to catch his. Got him in the calf hard. I still have shit-kicking boots on. Not as good as the SAF issue, but still steel-toed. He grunts, pulling distance. Now, I catch my breath.

Time to get up. Time for a real fight.

An incoming lunge with alternating closed and opening fists. I say, "Your trainer was Claude Marcel." He gets me with an open hand to nose.

"Fook, not my nose again," I moan around, blood and pain.

"Yeah. Full boar hand to hand. Feeling the pain, old man?" He hops around with show-off moves.

Fook, I think he broke a rib. Out of breath. "As a matter of fact, I am." Dodge, duck, spin. Gotta wait for my chances. The kid is too fast, and I am too screwed up. "You want to know who trained him?"

"You going to say you. Not possible. Claude is twice your age."

"Hell no. I was his punching bag," I say, cautiously stepping into his reach. "Which means…." His guard drops, letting curiosity defocus. My first throw catch's left temple perfectly. That made him stagger. I need to soften him more.

"Nice one, old man. That's your one move on me."

He comes in throwing moves like a well-trained professional. Just too crisp and perfect. SAF training in my day promoted discipline and, very importantly, spontaneity. Like, do something to throw things off.

"Hey, Good-looking," I say, dancing back to get distance, "did Claude show you this move?" Belt open. Fly down. Turn. Drop pants.

The room is dead quiet. Space quiet. Pants up. Ready for the fun part.

"You fooking old man. You die today," he says, coming at me like a wild bull on farms back in Italy. He didn't hide shock well.

Dad used to say to fight a bull, be a bull. I run right at him, drop to my knees and slide on broken vase parts. I can feel the shards slice through useless protection pants. We collide. Hard. Getting his leg with one hand while the other hand finds the man's spot.

He falters and falls forward, sliding face-first into the floor, clutching his blood-soaking crotch.

I say, "Nothing like slicing a set of testicles with real antique glass from Sicily." Looking at my own hand shows a deep cut. Well worth the exchange.

I hear Don Falcone yell, "Stop."

Who am I to argue at this point? Junior is on the floor, trying to keep the blood under control, wondering if he will ever use the meat again. I can't resist. "Hey, kid, next time, wear SAF crotch gear. Protect the jewels." I get a what look—not going to explain.

Don Falcone says, "Can you move, old man?" He says with a screwed-up sarcastic face. Yeah, I get to my feet. My knees are in rough shape. My nose is pumping blood like a broken damn. I have a headache the size of a ten-day hangover. And, sooner or later, I am going to have to spend an hour in the toilet. Two goons bring me a small white towel and a drink. Isn't going to be white for long.

"Thanks," I say, downing the drink. "What about him?"

"Cruel, Stone. I have to give you that. Nicking a man's balls. Finish," Don Falcone says.

"Really," I say, not intending to sound like an excited kid. "Can I have a weapon?"

"No," Don Falcone says.

It takes me a moment to get over to where the kid lays motionless in a puddle of blood. Face contorted in pain. He can barely speak around swelling lips. "Do it."

I do it. It's done. Working freelance while a member of SAF falls under Article 4. Forbidden. Every newbie has to learn the rules backward. SAF demanded complete dedication.

"What's next, Don Falcone? You want me to do the housekeeper?" I say. Now, I just want to die or leave. Either one is fine.

"I have 20 servants in my villa. You won't be killing any of them today. Allow me to invite you to sit here and take a break from injuries."

I sit. He's across from me. Goons are just over my shoulder. Should I worry about a wire around my neck?

"You will never work for another Family again. From this

day on until you die, preferably horribly, you are an open target. I place two million Yen contract over your head. Consider my magnificent mercy as respect for what you done for this Family and our Emperor. And yes, your father, may he rest in hell. I should make it 10 million, so all the crazies come for you. Run and hide, Stone," he says. His Standard English breaks down the more he goes on.

I say, trying to hide my surprise, "Okay. What's the catch, sir?"

He pauses with an odd look, kind of like he's afraid to speak. He says after a minute goes by. "I do not understand my thinking on this. Certainly, I have every right to just have you killed and send the body to Emperor Thaddeus. I should. A dream came to me, Stone. Do you dream, Stone? I wager the dead come to you every night. You know how it is near impossible to recall when you awaken." He pulls in closer. I'm so memorized by the intimacy I missed a chance to kill him. "I recall three words. I would throw those words away if it were not for the man that delivered them. Do you know who, Stone?"

Now he's so close we are almost nose to nose.

He whispers, "The image of the Christ. He says to me, plain and simple, spare the man. I woke up to my aid barging in, telling me little cockroach Jimmy had found you. Do you understand?" I think I hear cockroach Jimmy make scared cockroach sounds.

Well, talk about shivers all over. I am betting by the silence in the room, everyone is either in awe or internally laughing. I am tempted to go with pointing and mocking. I contain myself rather than spoil my chance to live.

Don Falcone abruptly gets up, apparently finished with me. He says, "My men will see you're cleaned up and wounds tended. Sober up. They will take you to a task I want completed before your retirement. Will you agree?"

"Sure. Agreed. Sounds a lot better than skin peeling."

He frowns. "No, that would be a kindness. I was thinking more like turning you over to contacts in the EOF. They reportedly have methods of torture that far outclass anything we have. Perhaps you have heard of the pain amplifiers?"

Yeah, that's the Don Falcone I know. I say, "I serve at the pleasure of the Families."

"Good. Go kill MIS Agent Saska just as planned." He stomps out of the room, mumbling something about going crazy.

"Fook," I say just as the lights go out.

21

MIS Agent Carol Saska
Pikes Homestead Apartments and Suites
Upper Level, City New Bourbon
World Caliadne

"KIA. PAY ATTENTION TO WHAT I SAY. ONLY THE THINGS YOU need to bring. Clothes, like tops, pants, your pinky sneakers, underwear, and no toys. Just your SatPad.

"Mommy, I need my wabbit," Kia moaned.

"Okay, that. Nothing else. Go finish now. I have to make some important calls. Okay, sweety. Please be good and please don't wake your brother. If he wakes, you can talk to him."

"Mommy, you know little Danny can't talk like me. I'm special." Kia says, face beaming without any concerns adults have.

What can a mother say to that? "Yes, Kia, you are my special little girl. I mean, big girl. Please do what I asked."

She trots off, mumbling about her wabbit, and Danny can't have one. Danny needs more than a wabbit to help him along.

I don't have time to stand here and feel sorry for myself. Or do I? Poor Danny, I'll feel sorry for you for as long as I live. It may not be a long life, just one with as much love as I have. "The Christ have mercy on me. Take care of my kids if they catch me."

SatCell in hand, dialing Jimmy's node again. I get a voice box. "Jimmy, please call me. I am sorry for what happened between us. Okay. Help me, and I'll help you. Call me back."

Next call, work if I still have work. The node routes me through encryption. This time I can tell it's off-world. Prime? Who knows what shadows have ears?

A female monotone voice says, "Node code?"

"Days and nights are warm," I say.

"Incorrect code," the monotone replies.

Fook, the code is changed. I'm out of the loop already. "Look, I'm Agent Carol Saska. I need to speak to the Sector Directory, Major Agent Upton, now. I need to talk with him now."

"Incorrect code," the monotone gone, replaced with irritation.

"Didn't you hear who I am? MIS Agent Carol Saska. World Caliadne. My Alpha code is A091998. I am compromised. I need to speak with Director Major...."

The node disconnects. So does my hope for the future. I am in deep and have no lifelines left. The SatCell rings its tone of Danny giggling. It makes me smile as a mother should, even in the worst moments.

"This is Saska," I say, trying to sound official. The ring must have unlocked emotions. I feel like water will flow.

"Agent Saska. Major Upton. You have a few minutes before the line tracer locks on you," he says. His voice is clear and steady.

"Nick, I am sorry, okay? My kids, Nick. I just want to get them clear," I say. Trying hard not to beg. My kids need a mother who can beg. Please, dear Christ, have mercy. I am sorry for doing wrong. Please save my kids.

"Saska, we know everything. Why should I help you? A traitor," he says about as harsh as possible. But he's talking to me. That's something.

"Damn it, Nick, you know why. We are from the same stars. They are not. The Emperor said so. Besides, I know where the intel originated. I know who was looking the other way. How far up does this go, Nick?"

"Saska. Carol, you know how this works. What's above you must remain in place. Forget anything you think you know. Destroy any evidence you think you have."

"Nick, c'mon. All my years of service. I did the dirty things without a bitch."

He interrupts, "And as you should. The oath you took isn't all about the job. You know it's the higher calling we all serve. Our Emperor knows nothing. The decisions are made where this darkness begins, just on the edge of light where we cannot understand the greater faith. Our Empire comes first. We are the true children of the Christ. Unfortunately, Saska, not all of the faithful understand that fact. Liberals think we should join the war all out. They think we are all the same children of the true Christ. The thought sickens me. Just as it does you. Let me get to the point for you, Saska, just because I used to like you, and yes, you served your Emperor and Church well, someone has to take the blame. Be a loyal person. Do what is right and know the Christ waits for you in Heaven. I have done one last favor for you, for the boy. I personally assigned a minor desk agent to find you. Perhaps you heard of her, Lieutenant Agent Carmen Torres. I bought you some time. Run, Saska."

And he's gone. What have I done? I did my duty for the Empire and Church. Now they want me to die to hide the guilty. No fooking way the Emperor does not know. Is he not the humble man directly connected to the Christ? No way the

Emperor is out of the loop on the biggest event for us since Earth fell.

How much time do I have? I know Nick won't turn me in right away. No way he wants his little boy harmed. Just disappear with the illegitimate child to keep his family from scandal. Bastard.

"Kia, hurry up," I yell. I can hear Danny sputtering awake. Soon he will need attention.

The knock on the door scares me. Where is my weapon? Damn it, Saska, remember the training. The knock increases in frequency.

Calm myself. It's a security building. No one gets in here without clearance unless your name is Stone. No, wait. If it's MIS or ODS agents, they have clearance. Got to pull myself together. Nick wouldn't do this. He said I have time.

Pressing the external door monitor. My eyes go pop.

"Stone?"

He's smiling. I do like that smile. Italians are all the same.

"Get in here," I say. Tears are at the dam's top level, ready to spill.

"Do not go for your service weapon," he says. I can't read his face. It's blank, without emotion.

"Okay. No weapon. How did you know where I am?"

"Carol, where else would you be? Home, packing to go into hiding. It's okay. Jimmy told me they want you out of the picture. You should get the security downstairs into more training. Wasn't a problem to walk in with a rogue pass and lots of clean Yen."

"Stone, they are calling me a traitor. I did what they asked me to do. No, they ordered me to do it," I say. A tear is leaking out. I don't want Stone to see me cry.

Baby Danny lets out a wild combination of cries and laughs with a side burp. "Stone, I need to handle Danny. You knew him as a baby with no name. Now he has a name. Too bad if it bothers you. Some of us have feelings," I heard my words, instantly regretting them. "I'm sorry, Stone. It's the pressure." True to form, the man didn't drop his happy grin.

"Danny is a good name. Irish. Knew a few in the SAF. Fooking good when pissed off at the enemy and not at me."

Just then, little miss tattletale shows up holding her wabbit. She says, "Who are you, mister? Do you work for my mommy? What's your name? Why are you so tall? Do you like my mommy?"

Stone laughs. He says with hands held up. "Wow. Yes, I work for your mommy, and she is a good boss. My name is Stone. I am tall because my father was tall. And, yes, I like your mommy. She is a very smart person." He looks at me and says, "Did I get all the questions? She should work for interrogation."

I throw him a shut-up look. "Kia, take one of the premade bottles from the cooler and feed your brother just like I taught you. I am right here, and I can see everything. Understood, young lady?"

"Yes, mommy. Please call me Princess Kia." She humps and goes about what I ask. Stone is just standing there like a statue.

"Why are you here, Stone?" I have to ask. I am terrified of the answer.

His face goes serious, smile long gone. His eyes glance around. Is he looking for anyone else? I say, "There is only me, you, and the two kids. Children, Stone."

He nods.

"Stone, listen to me. I did what I was told to do. Arrange to have the Imperium Queen assassinated. Not my fault you killed her husband, and now the Emperor and our worlds are nearing war with the Imperium and those devils. Jesus, Stone, sometimes I think we are cast back into the Middle Ages of old Earth with all this Queen, Knights, Empires, and dark devil powers."

"I understand, Saska, I really do. What do you think I did

in the SAF? Followed orders," he says. He takes off his sports jacket. He's got that cannon, his precious 440, strapped underarm. Easy pull, easy kill, he often bragged.

Now I am scared. More than ever. Not just for my life ending. For my children. They do not deserve to grow up in the Church's care.

The fear hits me like a chest punch. "Stone, my children. You can't." The words stick like glue in my throat.

He says softly. "No." I want to believe. For all the things that man has done. All the lives he's ended. I can't think he would kill my children and me. But his orders are orders, just like mine.

"You dream and talk. I hear the feelings in those sweats and cries," I say. "You're here for me. Do you want us on your conscience, too?"

His stare falters away. Like someone is getting his attention from somewhere else. He says, "My dreams are my Church penance. Believe it or not. I am human. This human needs a drink. Got anything? Don't tell me you don't drink; I know different."

"Yes. I'll get something. Give me a minute."

I come back with a small glass of cheap hard lemonade. He's not where I left him. He's looking into my room, where the kids are, lingering at the doorway. Danny is making half-sleepy sucking sounds on a river of milk.

Stone looks up with an odd face, like he seems to be intrigued. He says, "You breastfed the old Earth way. My mother did that. Some say it wasn't a good idea, given her addiction to RedFrost. Maybe it's why I am the way I am."

Princess Kia looks up at Stone like a hero for her to admire. She starts explaining every adventure she and wabbit have been on since creation.

"Kia, honey, Stone needs to leave soon. Wait with Danny. Don't let him drown in milk," I say, holding my voice still.

Stone tries to resist my pulling him away from the open

door. Getting him away gives me hope. Pushing him to the couch. He barely resists.

"Why are you the way you are?" I ask. I don't know why. Am I trying to reason with him, a natural-born conscienceless killer?

He thinks about it. I can tell by the frowned forehead. Damn, he is good-looking. "It's because I don't care much."

"No, Stone, you care. I can see it in you. You have a good heart."

He stands up and walks past me, taking the drink out of my hand. He says just under his breath, "Just because we fooked doesn't mean you know me."

I slap his face with everything I have. All the anger, fear, and regrets rolled into one slap. The sound reverberated around the entire apartment. It startled Kia. Danny didn't care; his world consists of milk and fingers.

Stone just looks at me, then walks back into the kitchen, empty glass in hand. Kia has perfect hearing. She asks. I say to Kia, "It's all okay, sweety. Mr. Stone and I are practicing for work. Please stay with Danny. Yell if you need me. I'll keep the door open so I can see you." She nods. It's not the first time she has witnessed me slapping a man.

"Stone, I am sorry. That comment was rude. I thought we had a thing."

He's sitting down. He says, "What the hell shit did you give me to drink? Now that's something that gets me upset. Never mind the slap. I had it coming."

"You are something else, Stone," I say, for some reason feeling a little less anxious.

He gives me that self-satisfied grin again. He says, looking at the empty glass as if it had the words, "They will have to space can you. You know that, right? Right or wrong for you, they will have no choice."

I know he is right. What I don't know is who sent him.

Nick was trying to give me time. "Who wants me gone, Stone?"

His anger flares. "C'mon Carol. Do I have to spell it out? Besides the Imperium, who I am sure was informed of a certain rogue MIS Agent, there are the Families who had the go-ahead from the Church. Wow, listen to all that spooky devil drama. How long did someone in the MIS hierarchy give you to get away? A few days? Carol, you are not a field agent; otherwise, you would know that two MIS heavy hitters are having trouble with most of their brains missing in the back alleyway. Compliments of me. And, yeah, I don't care if they have a dog at home that will miss them. The Church won't directly task anyone. They have the SAF for that. Upside on that one, it takes time to get SAF moving, but when they do, and if they are let loose, this entire apartment will go boom. That leaves the Families and me. As far as I can tell from my last encounter with Don Falcone, they want you in space just because they don't want to lose face. All of this is because they say I missed. I do not miss Carol. For the hundredth time, that man came out of nowhere. Must give him credit for putting his life out for the Queen. Anyway, two shots, end of night."

I say slowly because I mean it, "I am sorry, Stone. For all of this. For what you must do. I know if you don't, they will hunt you and kill you."

He frowns. I don't think I have ever seen this emotion on this heartless killer's face. "Stone, please, not my children."

He gets up. Tries to hide drawing the 440. "Please, no, not the children, Stone. I'll do anything. Please. I'll go in their stead. Willingly."

He says as if he's another man, "Like you will stop me. Stand aside." He pushes me to the ground. I get up. He punches my stomach. I can't breathe. Crawling after him. Where is my weapon? Maybe I can shoot him and then explain to Kia later it is all going to be okay.

"Stone…no. For the love of the Christ."

"The Christ can fook off," he says, kicking me away.

"Your mother, she wouldn't want you to do this," I say. I'm grasping at anything to get him on me. He hesitates. I get up. Catching my breath. "Stone, think."

"My mother was a whore and an addict. She did the best she could. Don't ever say that again."

Before I can say anything else, he walks away. My legs are iron. I stupidly laugh. He swats me away. I am a fly to him.

In my room. Kia is upset over something. She chooses to be oblivious to everything unless it's worth her curiosity. That's my blond daughter.

Stone stands there, 440 limp at his side. I am unable to speak. Dear Christ, please not this.

My lovely daughter sees the man who will kill her any second and then runs up to Stone. She says, her wabbit in hand, "My wabbit's eye fell out. Can you fix it, Mr. Stone?"

An eternity is passing by. Little girl tears are streaming down my daughter's face. So are mine. Stone is Stone. I drop to my knees just behind, trying to will the scene away, covering my mouth, holding back a scream.

I can't believe my eyes. He is holding the 440 behind his back. He wiggles it for me to see. I think he wants me to take it. I do. If the DNA safety is off, I can shoot him or lose my hand. Worth the risk. Think Carol, think. Oh, the Christ give me strength. The weapon shows the warning DNA off symbol. The 440 will let me pull the trigger.

He says in a calm voice, "Kia, let me have a look at the wabbit. Let's have a seat on the floor here. You can help me. Okay?"

I could end this man's life. Do the world everywhere a favor. Kill a killer. Why can't I do it?

We sit for almost thirty minutes while he gets that eye to hook back in. I've done it in less than two minutes. Is he stalling for time to think?

"There, it's fixed. Can't have a wabbit without two eyes, right?"

Kia is beyond happy hugging the revived wabbit. She swings her arms open and then wraps them around Stone's neck. A kiss as sloppy as children do plants on a reddening cheek. Big tough Stone had by a six-year-old.

Out in the living room, Stone isn't making eye contact with me. I must be careful.

He finally looks at me after a long wall of silence. I've got my emotions under control. I look back as a mother with children.

The door knock jolts the both of us back to a small apartment far from our thoughts of what to do next.

Stone looks at me. He says, "440, please."

I don't hesitate.

"Get ready to run," he says, then moves toward the door, 440 raised, his manly frame crouched, ready to take fire.

I know my kids are safe. I know he would die for them.

Stone is a good man, after all.

22

Stone
Pikes Homestead Apartments and Suites
Upper Level, City New Bourbon
World Caliadne

THE LITTLE GIRL, KIA, IS BREAKING MY HEART IN A WAY I NEVER thought possible. Can't let other people see this side of me. Hell, I don't want to see this side of me. She has her toy missing an eye. I never had toys unless a bat to beat other hostile Japanese boys away qualifies as a child's toy.

"Kia, let me have a look at the wabbit. Let's have a seat on the floor here. You can help me. Okay?"

I can't do it. I just can't. Don Falcone's threat is going to happen to her and me. Everyone can count on a threat from that black heart just as counting the sun comes up. It will happen. At least the order will go out off-world taking a day or two to get organized, giving us some time to run. The order will be for my end and hers and the two children, with lots of reward incentives. Maybe there is a chance of survival if I throw out cover fire for her.

Kia offers the toy for me to be a medic. Big sad eyes look

up. C'mon Carol, take the weapon. I'll need both hands. I can't let the kid see the weapon. The silencer is on. DNA off. Place the shot down my spine and limp I go. Sure, the kid would be upset, but fixable. Finally, Carol catches on. With both hands, I take the little injured toy, gently placing it on the floor while I kneel as if doing CPR. Is this what it's like to have a kid?

Today is a good day to die for a decent reason. Too bad Dad is waiting in hell, expecting a spectacular death by the only son we knew of. Being shot in the back isn't going to impress him. Too bad, Dad, I can't kill these kids. Carol knew the rules. The children are innocent. If I kill her, that won't save the kids. They will just end up being someone else's problem that the Don will have to kill to keep things quiet.

The thought hides behind other thoughts inside my head. It comes out to say something. You can't kill those children because you care. Your life isn't worth saving in place of two children. Children that one day can live, love, and have children better than you.

Sometimes I really don't like my thoughts, especially anything to do with a conscience.

Taking my time to fix this stuffed toy. Stuffed toys that don't act like some autonomous robot are rare. It takes a child's real imagination to create a personality behind something made completely from inanimate stuffing. How could anyone do harm to this child?

"There, it's fixed. Can't have a wabbit without two eyes, right?"

Kia is speechless. Somehow, I think that isn't her normal way. And she hugs me hard. What am I to do? Hug her back. This is screwing up my heartless bad guy image. Oh hell, she sloppy kisses me.

I can't look at her little eyes. She isn't crying now. A smile bigger than the sun itself fillers her face. That's a relief. I wonder what Selene would say. Would she ever forgive me? Does this day count as something good?

Carol and I need to talk. She needs to get far away. She should be able to construct alternate documents. I'll do what I can to distract the bad guys.

The firm door knock spooks me.

Carol says, "Stone? Who? This building is supposed to be secure." Her voice is wavering. Fear has pushed any training into the background. She checks the outside video.

"Do you know who that is?" I say, looking at the outside video image.

The man, not as tall as me, but thick looking under the black blazer, gray shirt, and classic tight informal jeans, smiles like we are all friends going to a restaurant. He says, "Pizza delivery from Happy Harry's Pizzeria."

Carol's face goes whiter than ever. She looks at me and says, "That's code word. He's either here to help or kill me."

"Who is he?"

"Black Taris," she says, barely able to speak.

"Ah, yeah, the ultimate Empire spooks. So dark that they don't even know who they are. We have attracted attention way up the food chain. If he were here to kill us, the rest of the SAF would already be here doing the killing. Let him in because he won't go away. Let's see what he has to say. I am right here, okay? Nothing is going to happen to the kids."

She nods reluctantly. I step away, just around the entrance hallway corner, out of direct sight. As long as the children stay put, I have field control. 440 in hand, full auto-ready.

Carol opens the door so slowly that I think we are in a horror movie. She says, "Who are you?"

"I'm not the pizza delivery man," he says. Sounds like a smart-ass. Spooks are usually smartasses. "Black Taris is who I represent. But you already figured that out. Glad you paid attention to training, Agent Carol Saska."

I hear Carol say, "Why are you here? I don't want to ask

again." Just then, the baby starts to wind up like jet engines. I know Carol doesn't have her service weapon on her. I saw it on the table, sticking out from under diapers. At another time, that would be funny.

He says, "If you need to tend the child, do so. The retired SAF Stone hiding can come out. I'll brief him. I cannot be here long, so be smart people; let's get this done before the bad guys get here." His voice is clear and commanding. I hear Carol do a tut and walk past me, her face frozen scared. Can't blame her. I hope she covertly picks up her weapon on the way.

I step out where he can see me, 440 leveled at his face. He smiles like a smartass spook. "We wait until she gets back," I say, carefully with my aim and angle. He has nowhere to go. The door is closed. A small, short hallway with only a closet to hide separated us. I'm all of a meter away. "I'll get two in you before you have any chance of reaching my position. One step backward, I can deliver two more. But you know that, Mr. Spook."

SAF made us newbies stand for hours holding various weapons leveled at a target. Special detectors measured how much the weapon weaved over time. First attempts were just practice. In the end, a serious shock hit the newbie's hand if weaving went out of bounds. After a few shocks, my hand can hold this weapon for hours. I think he knows it. Just standing there with hands folded in front, trying to piss me off with smugness.

Finally, Carol is back, out of breath, smelling like fowl baby smells.

"Tell me what, when, and where, then I'll lower the weapon. Otherwise, you die," I say. "And your real name. Just so that you know, I despise spooks." Ha, that seemed to rattle him a little anyway.

"You get my code name. That's it. Ravenhall." He pauses to make an announcement, "I'll get to the point. There are powers far above who are interested in letting you live, Agent Saska. Today is your last day as an MIS agent, and the only chance begins now to survive this day with your children. Certain powers are aware of the part you played in the botched assassination attempt on the Imperium Queen." He glances at me with a you-fooked-up-look. "These powers are generous and faithful to the true Church," he reaches inside his jacket.

"Nice and slow, there spook man. I'll pop you here and now," I say. Carol has smartly stayed out of the line of sight just behind me. Her face is somewhere between intrigued, scared, and happy.

Carol takes the documents to look over.

"Stone, oh my God. Passports. Travel documents. Credit accounts for the kids and me. Is this for real?"

"I must say, on a personal level, I have little use for you, Saska. If it were up to me, I would order you removed and left on a moon. As for your kids, a new home and loyal, god-fearing family would be best. Alas, I follow orders.

"Saska, do not share these details with Stone. When he is captured, a matter of time; despite how good he thinks he is, they will torture him. As tough as he is, sooner or later, he will give you up. If he doesn't know, he doesn't know.

"You will take nothing except what you have on. Leave any ID from your long-gone previous life. There is a travel ticket ready at the spaceport but use the local collection service to cover leaving. Having children should also help throw eyes off. Who would think an MIS agent fleeing justice would take her kids.

"I'll assume the two dead MIS Agents outside in the alley are the work of Stone. You will not have long before new eyes arrive. Your final destination, I do not know. More instructions are in that wafer chip. Do you know how to use that? Everything to do with this entire matter is now sealed and well hidden in the bowels of protective S-AI's just in case history needs to explain the past. As far as the rest of the empire knows, you disappeared. You are as close to Ghosted as possible. Do you understand the meaning of Ghosted?"

"Yes," Carol manages to spit out. I can hear sobs inside her chest, pushing hard to get out. "I am…I mean, I would be almost impossible to identify."

"Correct. Almost is the operative word. You must live quietly, never surfacing into daylight. Ghosted alone would qualify you for Church ex-communication and execution under the charge of treason. Your children will go to a Church run home. Certainly, you do know what that means for their lives."

He looks at me like I just crawled out of a toilet. "As for you, Stone. Nice shooting, you stupid ass. I have orders to kill you on sight. I bet I get a promotion putting down the great Stone. It seems you have the upper hand at this moment. Run away, Stone, like you have many times. Crawl back inside that bottle you seem to love more than life. I give you a few months before one of how many organizations get you. Jesus, how did you manage to shoot the wrong person? Shame."

Carol catch's my eye. She says, "Don't do it, Stone. Let it go for the sake of my kids."

Just then, two little arms grab my leg. Little Kia looking up at me with a face of curiosity. She says in her girly voice, "No shooting guns inside the house. I am a Queen. You have to do what I say." Don't know why that sent a chill down my dumb backside. Carol isn't sure if she should laugh or scream. Spooky man gives me a very strange look. Mother used to say from the mouth of children, except that was more like stopping my nasty name-calling of the Johns.

"Suffice to say, I am no longer here. Have a nice life. You, Stone, can burn in hell." He turns away, opens the door, then says over a shoulder, "Always do what the Queen says, Stone." And he's gone.

"Damn it. I hate it when someone gets the last word in," I

say. What I wanted to say is that one day I would kill him just because he's annoying, but I'll keep that to myself. Carol has enough to deal with.

Carol muses, "Isn't that the truth."

Twenty minutes later, I am escorting her to the spaceport collection terminal. We take a transporter to keep it low. Illegal but overlooked. No one will expect that. I am all eyes everywhere, looking for any target. Kia is babbling like kids do. Little Danny is having a drink from the boob fountain. The driver knows to keep looking forward once I showed him my big fist in his little multi-ringed nose.

Getting to the upper-level collection station is safely done. I say, "I can't follow you through security. A hat, high collar, isn't good enough to hide my wanted ass. I think you are safe. Things change. Politics change."

The overhead PA is announcing collecting calls for her boarding the air-bus. From here, she and the kids will land at the proper spaceport and then shuttle up to a liner.

Kia pulls on my arm. Seems my arm is connected to my heart. I pick her up into a surprise hug from a six-year-old. She says nothing. Hugs are thousands of words, so Mother told me. Dad always said hugs are for girls.

"What are you going to do, Stone?" Carol says.

"Do not worry about me. SAF to the core. I can take care of myself. Been doing it since birth. Just get going and stay away. Don't relax. When you can, make other plans to hide. I'll do what I can to keep them interested in me."

She seems to want to argue. She kisses her hand instead, then places it on my cheek. Well, seeing as I was to kill her and the kids, it's the best I'll get for a goodbye.

She says, "How do I thank you?"

I nod. "I didn't do anything."

She smiles and says, "Yes, you did. You fixed Kia's stuffed toy. Before I go, would you have?"

I know what she is asking. I try to look away, but her eyes

are like anchors holding me still. "For a microsecond, I could have. A voice in my head said no. Good enough answer?"

"Keep listening to that voice," she says.

We stare at each other, not knowing how to end.

After a full minute, I say, "Goodbye, Saska."

She is gone without a word, carrying one kid, the other in tow. I feel empty. I see a bar nearby. Time to drown myself in self-centered despair. Been a long while since I bar-hopped on the upper level. In those good days, Don Falcone paid the bills.

I barely get a couple down when the face looking at me from the other side of this swanky tavern fails to look inconspicuous.

I know why he is here. I just don't know who he is working for.

23

IN AN HOUR, EX-MIS AGENT CAROL SASKA AND THE KIDS WILL be at the spaceport on a shuttle off-world, a destination unknown to me. Good luck, Agent Carol Saska. Hope I never see you again. Hope you appreciate it. She should be okay. She is a desk spook. Even desk spooks have their way of hiding in plain sight. The blowback from not canning her and kids spells the end for me. Forever on the run for me. Being honest with myself, I won't last that long because the fight is withering. But I will take down as many as possible. What am I turning into?

Left the bar just a little bit buzzed around the edges.

This city's upper level is bigger than I expected to walk around the outer parameter. Dumb idea to try stacking cities but no surprise for greedy politicians. If I recall local history, it was the original settlers who thought more people would migrate to one of the first truly habitable worlds, so why not keep the forests pristine by building cities on levels? Bad idea.

Lots of people walk around because, for once, it's not raining in some fashion. Lots of green spaces and lots of stores of things everyone wants as long as one has the credits and only credits. No illegal Yen flowing freely up here. It's clean and tidy. Perfect narrow streets. Almost no ground traffic, as everything is air-based and so tightly controlled. Even the air smells better. Lots of legal credits or who you know to get a small upper-level apartment.

Let's see if I am followed by the bar fella staring at me. Not a spook. Never been one, and I am not interested in becoming one. Even so, an amateur should be able to spot anything suspicious, like the same face many times. Can't remember the name of a retired spook trainer who told us if we are behind lines, worried over being followed, then simply accept one of two eventualities; you're going to die very soon, or you're just paranoid. I think both are applicable to my sorry ass.

I need people around me until some sort of plan comes to mind. I need more intel. How many and who is on me? Look for familiar faces, eyes hidden behind any kind of reflective glasses. Hot dog stands that don't make sense. That list is far too long to manage. No sense in trying to avoid confrontation. I doubt anyone will try much up here. Too snooty. Lots of so-called police that are pretty much community-paid, meaning don't bite the hand that scratches your back. Anastasi stay on the ground level, where they belong, unless there is serious reason to come up to dirty the streets.

I drank way too much in the last bar. Not at the top of my performance. Or was it too much? Takes the edge off. Less worry about staying alive and more about not thinking about it. Checking 440. Yep, still there. Two spare clips. All high velocity, middle-grade armor piercing. Wish I had some poppers. A multi-head rocket launcher too. Hell, a P-Tank. Why not?

Naw, I have been in far worse condition many times before. I should have drunk more. Won't feel pain as bad. It's time to take this downstairs to the ground and get dirty. I'm betting from the odd looks, simpler faces, and silly places normal people never stop to read a SatCell, like standing by a smelly dog poop deposit. I have at least five followers. One is definitely armed for certain, judging by a badly placed back belt holster. Police see that, and all hell and thunder will happen. I must be getting better at this anti-spook stuff.

I wish I had a SatCell. I wish I knew how to use a SatCell. Makes calling a taxi a lot easier. Old ladies are always kind, right?

"Excuse me, can I ask you for a favor?" I ask a gray curly-haired lady parked casually on a bench and knitting what looks like the longest scarf ever. If I had a grandmother, this one looks perfect. She even has a grandma-looking dress and black shoes, complete with a wide-brimmed straw hat with a purple bow. Oh, and the awful broach. Looks like a dead thing with colored stripes.

Her voice is strong for the number of age wrinkles. "What can I do for you, young man?"

"I need an air-taxi to pick me up. Need to go to the surface for business," I say. I hope she can't smell the booze. I must reek. It is hitting me hard now, trying not to weave back and forth. Good thing for sun shield eyewear. Kind of feeling a little sick.

"Well, as a God-fearing follower of the Christ, I will be happy to call for you. You look a little flushed. Must not be feeling well with all this wonderful sunlight. It is a large day, would you not agree? I am sure you would. Shall I choose a company? Yes, I will, of course," she says, comfortably answering her own questions.

All I can do is smile. Wow, whatever was in those drinks is

kicking my ass—shutting down one eye to avoid duplicate old ladies. I am a professional killer with a degree in drinking. Feeling like I'm 14 on my first drunk all over again.

"You do not look well, young man. Are you not taking good care of yourself? You must think about that if you want to be my age. Do you know how old I am? 101 years. Yes, I am. You, young man, best be careful with your time." She makes the call. I'm working on not falling over from vertigo.

The air-taxi sets down on a nearby curb outside the little park. I see the roof lights flashing.

"I best be going. Thank you for your help," I say, trying to walk away. She reaches for a bony hand for mine. I don't pull away.

It feels like ice. Like she's dead but still alive. A shiver does its thing up the backside. Her blue eyes are alive for 101 years old. I wonder if they are implants.

"That's one hell of a grip," I say. And it is. She must have done serious physical labor years ago.

"Be healthy," she says, finally letting go. I swear my hand is numb. "I hope we meet again. Don't forget old Hazel."

The air-taxi uses an air horn to tell everyone nearby the driver does not like to wait. Between blasts from the asshat driver, I hear the old woman yell, "Sober up, Stone."

From the backseat, I say, "Lower level. Quickly. Any place near a mall, a motel, and a booze supply. You choose. Make it good for a tip."

The driver, a woman, grunts, teeth clenched, "Yeah."

I am so tempted to smack that snarly face. Ugly face. Yeah, very ugly face. Not letting my mind go to what the rest of her looks like or risk puking this back seat full to the windows with industrial chunks.

Off we go. Wow, wait a minute. Both eyes are working normally. The head is clear. What happened to the nice alcoholic haze I had? Damnit, that cost lots of credits I don't have. I need lots to drink more.

"Hazel? Where did I hear that name before?" I say out loud.

Ugly driver says, "What name?" She's giving me seriously weird looks. Like, do we know each other? No way I get into bed with that. Suddenly the safety glass between the passenger and driver zips across and goes no see-through black.

I should be worried.

I should have realized I overdid the drinking thing at the worst time.

I should have asked the polite, interesting centenarian woman how she knew my name.

24

WHEN AN AIR-TAXI DRIVER FEELS THREATENED BY A PROBLEM passenger, they can use the security features designed to isolate the passenger until assistance arrives. Projectile-proof driver-passenger divider, same for the small side windows, no back window, and door auto-locked. Rumors have it that some unscrupulous drivers have self-defense built-in, like low-impact seat shocks to immobilize passengers. Trying to hover my ass over the seat isn't working. The backseat was now a prison, and I'd rather die than be in a cell, one of my worst fears.

Not all air-taxis have the feature. Of course, my luck, a paranoid driver, or is the cab paranoid? Either way getting out of this air-taxi prison anytime soon is completely utterly dependent on when the security system stands down. Tagging her as target Ms. Ugly. Now that I am sober and pissed off, as soon as the door opens, out comes grumpy bear. Thanks, Mother, for that disturbing bedtime story.

Dunno where I am exactly. Senses of direction and time with all-out acceleration pressing me into the seat should put me well outside the city. Can't be sure. It feels like I'm northeast, possibly along the coast. Well, for sure, not going to the Anastasi station for interrogation. This is about whoever wants to isolate and terminate. I bet the sour face back in the bar has something to do with it, maybe a scout or someone too slow to get to me first.

Ugh, we must be descending. My guts just hit the ceiling. Twisting around like lining up for a landing spot that's not wide-open space. This is going to get interesting. Time 440 woke up.

Is it dead?

These weapons have power sources that last for a decade. No way 440 can be dead. Yet, nothing. Trying diagnostics. Nothing.

No good.

A thump rattles my teeth. The taxi landed on a slight incline to my right. Sliding over to that door and use gravity to help me spring out. No weapon means only hands and big feet. If I see an easy target, then it's knuckle time with a solid crotch kick.

The other side door opens. The driver's unladylike hoarse voice calls out, "Get out."

Well, it was a good idea. Sliding to the open side. Gingerly legs out first, gravity making it a non-graceful exit, right into lots of hot, temporarily blinding sunlight.

The driver says, all giddily like, "Thanks for flying Omicron Air Taxi Service."

"Hilarious," I say. Eyes are finally focusing. A quick scan around tells me a forest, a deep forest. Small clearing barely fitting much more than an air-taxi or two. Can't see far past brush and huge thick-leafed Caliadne trees. Upside, it's not raining. Downside, it's hot and muggy, threatening to down-pour, making everything moist. Won't matter, seeing as I am here to be killed or kill first.

The driver is nothing but an ugly short woman with a man-hating attitude written all over her hook nose and blotchy face. Not that super small people are all bad; it's when they go out of the way to blame me like I did it. The worst kind when armed. Lots of reasons to hate good-looking men like me. For anyone else, I would try to get warm with her. Then kill her out of mercy.

She pulls out a long barrel western-style called a 45. Old as the star system. Prone to easy mistakes in the wrong hands. Wrong little hands of ugly women.

"Point that old projectile away from me. If you're after money, I haven't much left for Yen. Credit hookups from the middle of this nowhere forest will be dependent on a close NAVSAT, and they don't bother with the wild outdoors. So, this can't be a robbery. Care to tell me who we are waiting for because you are not the hired gun. Which brings me to an important point for you, ugly woman. Someone who wants me isn't going to give whatever they said they would pay, let alone let you live to dream of a facelift."

I just can't help myself sometimes. That made Ms. Ugly mad. Gritting teeth, eyes wide, and as expected, the old weapon raises to level at my groin.

Her forehead suddenly has a red dot just as brains fly out the back. She crumples into a bed of dead leaves. Glad her finger didn't twitch away my balls.

I say, "Told ya." Looking around slowly for whoever took the shot to thank them and hopefully talk myself out or at least give a good fight to the death. If I was to be dead, I'd be talking to Dad right now.

A mild-toned male voice from behind—bad guys always manage to sneak up from behind—and says, "Sorry about making a mess of her. She was not authorized to act."

"No worries, you did mankind a favor," I say cheerfully. Hoping to get a sense of humor from this guy. I feel the presence getting closer, yet I can't hear any footsteps. This forest has a deep carpet of crunchy things like leaves and twigs. I slowly raise my hands to shoulder height. Best location for self-defense and looking passive at the same time.

"I see you have done this before. Let us go one step further. Please bend to your knees and place those dangerous hands behind the head. Do not move quickly or attempt to move without my explicit permission. In my hand, I hold a weapon that will cause extreme pain before death comes as mercy. Understand?"

I nod slowly. Must admit, the weapon sounds like I want one. Wonder if it's DNA locked. Whatever it is, it's hi-tech, and I'm guessing not Earth human made.

I see at my eye level an odd hexagon-shaped muzzle appears in my peripheral only inches away. It's more like a narrow silver-looking short rod attached to a body of dull black featureless metal held in a tanned long-fingered hand, with multicolored fingernails. That fad comes and goes. But that tells me he is soft. Maybe not military. He moves around me to stand a few feet away.

"May I hazard a guess you have never seen a weapon like this, have you, Stone?" The voice doesn't fit the man. He is at least my height, weight, and young face blood-red crew-cut hair. Dressed like a businessman from upper levels in the city in a pressed suit is making me jealous.

"Nope. Can I hold it, just for a second?"

He frowns. Bet he's not into humor. He stands in front of me, too far to lunge. Sun is at his back, making it hard to focus on depth. He says, "We will have a conversation. You will live. I will live. All is well. You will go home under a rock. Next time we meet, you will die, most horribly. I may allow you to ask a question only if the question is within my operational parameters. Understood?"

The interesting weapon remains pointed at me. Although, I think it won't matter where it hits when it goes off. The target suffers and then dies in a bad way.

"Imperium, or what's their name?" I ask.

That didn't go over well. The weapon lights up just as a shock peals through me like a lightning strike. I can't move, and it hurts like fook.

"That, Stone, is the lowest setting. Just to ensure my safety and your cooperation, I have reset to a higher setting. I suggest you do not wish to discover the level."

It takes a few seconds to nod my head.

"Let me begin. My true name is unimportant. I am an agent for the Empire of the Fathers. Our Fathers wish to send you greetings."

My mouth isn't working properly. I manage to say between grinding teeth, "Tell them to fook themselves. Thanks."

Not sure how long I've been on the ground convulsing, drooling while planning how the fook I am going to kill this gloating asshole from space. He didn't fulfill his promise to kill me, so I am still a commodity for something.

Wish I wasn't sober.

Looking up, I get a face full of tangy rain.

"Gotta love the weather, right?" I say.

25

Stone
Outside City New Bourbon
Somewhere in Middle Estonia Territory.
World Caliadne

"STONE, WILL YOU NOW KEEP YOUR COMMENTS RESPECTFUL? I cannot have you speaking terrible words directed at the Fathers. They are our true salvation, to whom we owe our existence, not the man of imagination you call Christ. Please understand, I have all day, as your saying goes. No other human misses you. You would not survive this hostile forest in your current condition. Do we have an understanding?"

I nod yes. I would cross a finger or two if I could get them to move. This is right up there in pain levels with wands we use on uncooperative animals and people who act like animals.

"Go ahead," I sputter out. Snot is flowing so fast makes me wonder where it's stored.

"Very good. My purpose here is to bring thoughts of the Fathers. The Empire wishes to extend its appreciation for you dispensing of the man called Knight Rogan."

Silence for a few moments while he stands there, all smug looking, holding that fooking weapon. Love to shove that up his ass, assuming those people have holes.

"That's it? Drag me all the way out here into the middle of some prehistoric forest no one gives a crap about to tell me those Fathers are happy I killed the wrong person? Oh, and kill the world's ugliest taxi driver?"

"That is partly correct," he says. "I killed the ugly woman."

Silence again for a few moments.

"So, what's next? Are we going to take a shower and clean me up?"

He smiles at that. He says, "Homosexuality is not required in our worlds. Everyone has a proper place and purpose."

Now I am curious. Getting back to my knees and hands locked position, I ask, "What about sex?"

"Ah, yes. The act of copulation. Our people, with the Father's blessing, may practice such as frequently and safely as wished. Of course, only when not in the Fathers' service and under close observation to prevent improper feelings. Further to that, when approved, females may earn the designation to bear a child. Otherwise, all children spring from birthing centers. We are a proper and organized society. If only your government recognized this fact, the human race would benefit greatly."

So much to take apart in that. I say, "First of all, women get to choose. Second, sex isn't dirty with or without feelings. I prefer none, but it's a choice free people make. Third, birthing centers? Seriously, for all our faults, we learned children need parents to grow up nice. Look at me for the bad example. Forth, you lot are barely human. Look like us. Smell like us. I assume bleeds red like us. But no way I call you murderous bastards human. You fooks wiped out my world." I stop there, not that I couldn't go on. Ran out of breath.

"Stone, you are quite misinformed. Such as the so-called

Imperium are fond of saying that they are the only true branch of humanity. However, the history of our original galaxy proves otherwise. The history we could provide you with eye-opening education. The Fathers bring solidarity, balance, organization, personal worth, and the warmth of a self-sufficient society filled with like-minded humans. Finally, we have reached a level of advancement not driven by emotions that bring only pain and suffering. Everyone has a purpose, a long healthy life, everything they need to blossom as men and women should."

"You make it sound like a religion," I say. I'm watching for that cursed weapon to pan away from me.

"Stone, please do not insult our society. We shed ourselves of religion a thousand years past. This chain your people shackle around your necks greatly restricts forward movement in a universe tended for open minds."

"Well, I'll agree with you on that. Okay, I accept their thanks for a job done. What's next?"

"Yes," he straightens up as if he's going to say something that only gods should hear. "On behalf of the Empire of the Fathers, we extend you, Stone Giacalone, the privilege of citizenship. Of course, this will come with many benefits, such as extended life, weapons even you cannot fathom, and access to missions tailored to your skill sets. In addition, you will enjoy protection from those who wish your death, a list quite long. We ask for your loyalty for life. A few stipulations you must refrain from alcohol, mood-altering drugs, and unapproved sexual contact."

I laugh without thinking. "Really, no sex?"

He frowns like he just stepped in dog crap.

"What if I decline?"

"Our society always allows a choice in freedom of will," he says, totally blank-faced. I know what that means. He has to kill me if I say no.

"Okay. Sign me up. Time for a change of life for me. Like

you said, the list is long. The SAF doesn't like me. The Families want me dead. I am betting the Imperium would love to get their pagan hands on me. My liver needs work. Drugs make my head hurt. I'd be happy to fill out forms to get started. So, yeah, take me."

He smiles like he's won the EOF lottery. I wonder if they would give him a medal for getting the famous killer of Knight Rogan. "So, what's next? Do I sign somewhere?"

Out of a breast pocket, he pulls out a small dull silver gadget about the size of Dad's pillbox. He says, "Press a thump on this device. It will register your DNA and code a new citizen number that will mark you for life." He extends a fingertip of a well-cultured hand. I reach slowly, like my arm isn't suddenly long enough. He reaches, bending, stretching more with a masked grunt. My fingers touch the warm box. It's one of those moments where a fumble occurs. In nature, it is quite common. It happens when two people misjudge distances and expect the other to have control. Maybe his branch of humanity hasn't thought of that. The little dull silver box slips away and falls in slow motion on the moist ground where the waiting leaves and debris gobble it up.

"Oops," I say as innocently as possible.

He says something in some other language. I guess it must be EOF talk. Then he reaches down to snap the box up.

It's a glorious moment for me. Off my legs into the air. Headfirst into a chest of a bureaucrat. I know that because there is no way a well-defined military man would ever fall for this trick, let alone trust for a moment on a deadly prisoner like me. The awesome weapon merrily bounces away, out of reach for both of us.

I'm on him. My knuckles go raw from punches. At first, his hand blocks, but I am too strong and fast pumped with I want to kill-you-adrenaline. I feel a snap as one of my fingers breaks on what was a nose. Yeah, they bleed red, just like us. Lots of blood.

Not one word gets out of his mouth.

Looking down at a face long lost to everything broken and pulped, I say, "Like I would ever join your sorry ass Empire. You killed my world. I will kill yours if I ever get the chance."

I had to go pee, so I did. He didn't mind.

Now, for the awesome weapon. Do I dare touch it? Yes, damn sure. I pick it up, point it at the dead man, and press, knowing it could be a colossal mistake. And nothing happens. Ten minutes of messing with it. Nothing. Gonna guess here and figure it's tied to the dead EOF man's hand. Putting the weapon in a stiffing hand. Nothing. Bah, it's broken.

Now to get back to civilization. Well, look, there is an air-taxi that I have no idea how to use.

Yes, a SatCell on the dead taxi driver. Nothing of value on the dead EOF fella. Not touching that box. Taking a few leaves to pick it up and toss it inside the air-taxi. And inside goes his dead ass and her ugly taxi driver's body. These air cars are not hard to explode when one knows how, and they burn hot right down to bits of hybrid metals. Flesh and bones do not last. Good thing SAF showed us how. Tossing in the broken weapon. I hesitate. What if it has a power cell that is allergic to heat? Naw, who cares?

I call Jimmy on the only number I ever can remember, except for Selene, but she isn't talking to me. The fire roaring from the overheated control systems in the air-taxi will work as a flag of where to find me. Black smoke shoots up from seriously red flames making for a flag-waving here I am.

First thing he says is, "I told you to forget me."

I say, "You've said that a couple of times, yet here you are answering the call. Miss me already?"

Jimmy arrives an hour later, all pissed-looking. The bugs are chewing on me. They must smell the blood.

"I want you to understand we are through, and I mean it this time. Not fooking around, Stone. You are far too hot to touch," he says, looking at the burning taxi. "Should I ask what and who?"

"Naw, nothing too big. Just the world's ugliest woman trying to have unwelcomed sex with me in the woods. She got rough. I reciprocated. Story over. How about you buy me some food and booze, and I'll thank you lots?"

"Stone, you are a sick man."

"I'll take that as a yes. Can I get some medical help? My finger is broken," I say, holding up a finger that isn't pointing anywhere near the right direction. Can't miss the missing skin on the bone showing metal reinforced knuckles.

Jimmy takes one look, does a mock gag, then says, "Not interested in how that happened."

"And you call me sick?" I say. Sometimes Jimmy is okay. Most of the time, I just want to put his ass in space. I guess we have a like-hate relationship.

Two minutes later, the air car bounces up and down and sideways by a concussion wave. Looking back where Jimmy picked me up, we see a tiny cloud of angry black stuff shooting up.

Jimmy says, "What the fook was that?"

I say, "An allergic reaction."

26

Stone
Somewhere
City New Bourbon
World Caliadne

I CAN'T REMEMBER HOW LONG IT'S BEEN SINCE THE EOF AGENT made that offer to spy and kill for them. The Agent is dead, and I am, well, almost.

Time for a life recount.

How many motels, drinking buddy couches, alleyways, and para-cardboard boxes have I slept in? Uncountable. No idea how many bars I've partied like a fish fought anyone by breaking bones and egos', then thrown out, landing in someone's puke. Can't afford RedFrost in any form anymore, but there is always a second choice. Little pills of all kinds.

How much money do I have left? None. All my credit accounts were closed by the government. The clothes on my back are all I own, and they are not much. Not even a gun. Sold 440 for couple hundred Yen. Felt like I lopped off a hand. Can't remember if I disengaged the DNA safety. Oh well, too bad for the new owner.

Now for the best and most important statistic, how many people have I sent to rest in a can floating in space, burned away, or left in an alley under garbage? Only two, and that was in self-defense. Should not have tried to take my boots and slander my mother at the same time. Okay, being honest with myself. There were four stupid Family goons with little talent. One other tried me with a distance shot. How he missed, I'll never know. I did everything but wear a target that said, kill me, please.

For the first time, I have no idea what day it is. Where I am is easy to know by the dankness, down by the original docks, where the first settlers launched wooden boats. That didn't work out well. No one bothered to ask the sea monsters if it was okay. The sea monsters are gone now. Relics from another age, just like me.

So, while I am plodding along, hungover from breathing aerosol-alcohol like the worst down and out do when liquid isn't available. I should confess to the unknown gods; yes, I am trying to kill myself. For the fourth time. No one really wants me dead, or I be dead by now with this many enemies. Even Dad should be proud of me for how many people want me dead.

What a curse. Stuck alive in a living hell.

I had lots of time to think about my life. All the things that have happened. I don't believe in heaven, but just to be playing both sides, what have I done to warrant at least a hearing at the gates of heaven?

Let's see. I spared some lives along the way. I never killed children. Well, except for a few that came with weapons to kill me, and they were older teenagers. In fact, there was a good reason for all kills. Okay, maybe not that guy with the mother jokes. Accidents will happen. Oh, what about what's her name, Agent Saska? I let her and her kids live. That has to count for something. Maybe it will add up to get me a better seat in hell.

This is a good spot on this pier. No one around. The area is abandoned, buildings are slated for removal, and the gray, wet fog makes me invisible. The water is cold as always, choppy with deep currents and full sets of fish teeth that will clean up. Dangling legs over the pier edge like Selene and me aboard her father's yacht. The fog smells like the sea. Not like back on Earth. That sea smell with talkative Selene and brave Seagulls is something I've never forgotten.

Ah, Selene. What can I say? You were the best. More than this man ever deserved. I hope you are okay. I don't know what love is, so the SAF head shrinks told me. No conscience, they said. No feelings of right or wrong. I disagree. I know what right is. I prefer to do the wrong because I was born this way and groomed this way since Mother brought me home to meet her new John, the one that introduced her to drugs and me to belt whippings. That piece of human waste is dead. Made sure of that.

Going to not think about the things I slept with. It's a wonder my parts haven't melted off.

And Dad, I can't leave you out of this mini confession, can I? Actually, you tried hard, as in how to do family business, which was what, Dad? Yeah, let's not go there. Most boys are proud to lose their virginity in their teenage years. I was pronounced a man at thirteen for killing a rival Family bad guy. Yeah, I didn't make the kill shot, but no one knew that, did they, Dad?

The dreams are the last straw. One more nightmare of people I have canned, dragons that cook me alive, and that fooking Queen, and I go mad. Not a way to end up in a metal box having a guy wipe my ass for me.

I am never going to be sorry for killing her husband, the Knight Rogan they called him. Last one of his kind, they said. Who cares, I say. Useless waste of space. All things come to an end, even medieval wanna-be Knights in shining armor.

Here I sit. Ready to get this sad excuse for life over. No

regrets. No feeling sorry for myself. No way I apologized. I am at the bottom of life. I may as well be at the bottom of the bay. Okay, I won't be at the bottom. Even my alcohol-soaked body will float while fish enjoy a meal.

A voice echoes around the pier bouncing off gray sticky fog yells, "Hey, you."

It can't be security. I yell back, "Fook off or die."

"Are you not the great Stone?" the voice, a female, yells. She is getting closer. I am intrigued by the phrase, 'great.'

"Yeah. Over here. If you're here to kill me, you can do it. I'm ready."

The figure slips silently out of the fog. Not bad looking, as far as I can tell, under the dark buttoned-up overcoat. Long hair, brown, big eyes, and a happy smile.

"Glad I found you," she says, coming right up and sitting beside me like we are kids.

"I think I am also glad," I say. "I have no money. Nothing of value. Was just about to feed the fish."

"I saw you at McMurphy's last night. The bar, remember?"

"I was at a bar last night?"

"Yeah, you danced with me. Promised me another date tonight."

"I did?"

She laughs. "Silly man. C'mon, let's head over there now. They have a special going on. I won't let you get into a fight and be thrown out."

"I got into a fight?"

She pats me on the head. "C'mon. My treat."

"What's your name? I never ask for names, but I dunno, today is different."

She smiles and says, "Vicky."

I think she's lying. Don't care.

It's been how long? Twelve hours. Hard sex, moderate drinking, and endless talking. That was just in the bar. Somewhere near city docks, we both pass out on a bed made of nails, her on top of another female I had never seen before. It's well into the night, like near 3 am, so my internal clock says, but I wouldn't trust that too far. Thinking is hard. Did she say she had work for me? Or was that driven by wishful hope for a reason to keep going? Looking myself in the bathroom mirror that has puked on it. Now, that's gross. I look gross. Sick. Lines everywhere. Badly covered scars. One eye isn't opening all the way. Maybe it's telling it's had enough. My guts hurt; been shitting a river of brown fluid, my knuckles are raw to the bone, a few exposing metal plates from previous injuries. That's not as bad as what I am seeing inside those eyes mother used to stare into. Not sure she saw anything, given the amount of RedFrost in her blood. It's what I don't see that used to scare me.

I cant see why I keep on going anymore. Shooting and killing isn't what it used to be. It was me, what I live for. Or what I used to love to do.

"Fook this," I say to my haggard face. "Its time to take a walk."

The docks on the shoreline are dead quiet. As usual, it rained a flood and then swept in fog from the bay. Ships tied up here and there, all quiet and no one around. Funny, we still use ships to move some things. I guess that past won't go away. Good old-fashioned fishing off these docks. Dad and I used to fish a long back on Earth, off piers that went way out into the deeper waters. That was a good time.

I miss him sometimes. Such an odd feeling to miss someone. Just like those times we sat on the edge looking into the dark waters he would tell me about his jobs he did for the Families. Good times. I know he is in hell, if there is one. Said he would wait for me there.

Not a bad idea, really.

"Damn, my head hurts," I say. A seabird swoops over top. "You shit on me I'll find you." Trying to eyeball the fooker as it swoops back again. I feel my body slide forward. Another few inches and splash, I'm on my way to Dad.

A voice from all around struggles through pea soup fog to reach my ears. I am hearing things.

"Fook off, bird." I swipe at the bird as it squawks bird swear words at me. My ass slips over the edge. Is the bird holding me? The waves lap at the edge, trying to pull me down. One more second, and it's all over. Stone is no more. Fook you world.

Then weightless. Am I falling?

Rough hands grab my arms.

Suddenly, the bird speaks. "Got you, you stupid fook. You're not going to get away that easy."

Everything goes white, then black. A female voice says, "Go to sleep, Stone. You're not going to hell just yet." I know the voice, it's that Vicky thing.

I dream of terrifying fire-breathing dragons.

<u>**GET FREE NOVELLAS AND STORIES**</u>

Writing is my passion. Meeting new people is part of that passion. I would like to warmly invite you to join my mailing list called Stones Retirement Club. When I have a new book out in the Armsman series, or in the new series under development titled *Chronicles Of Rath*, and other short stories, plus release specials (Hardcovers, etc), then please click the link below. If you have questions, please free to contact me at max@mcchamberlain.com

For joining, I will send you a few free things to read. (eBooks)
1. A complete set of the Prequels for the Armsman series
2. Special Chapters of Doragon (Before Armsman was born)
3. Classified records of Sergeant Stone (Retired)
4. Short Stories in the Armsman Universe.
5. Chapters from Chronicles of Rath.
6. Assortment of short stories.
Here is the link: mcchamberlain.com
Thank you!

**Please note: Prequel I,II,III
are available FREE as ebooks. You can download them
anytime. Please join Stones Retirement Club to receive your
ebook collection at** mcchamberlain.com.
**If you wish printed copies, I can provide them for a small
cost. Please email me directly for the how-to at admin@
fussputterpress.com**

Also by MC Chamberlain
ARMSMAN SERIES
Rescue: Ambassador – Book III

<u>*AVAILABLITY TBD*</u>

Kidnapped by the Empire of the Fathers, agents whisk Ambassador McGuinness away, hiding the sage old man deep inside captured territory.

The Imperium tasks Armsman Stone to rescue the Ambassador before it's too late and before the tortured man gives away war secrets. **Stone soon learns the rescue is not what he was told.**

He teams up with an Imperium female solder. For a moment, **Stone feels something** he refuses to remember since Selene died in his arms. Will he let the soldier die to save the Ambassador? If Stone isn't careful, could he fall in love? Can he get to the Ambassador in time before the EOF discover the rescue team? Stone must move quickly before the Ambassador breaks.

Just as Stone thinks nothing worse can happen, an assassin strikes with an arrow to the heart from the last person he imagined. **Should he kill Princess Eden or let her live?**

Join Stones Retirement Club to receive word when Armsman Stone's adventures hit the shelves and other new

work just for you. Go to mcchamberlain.com/stone. You will receive 3 FREE prequels (ebooks 90K+ Words).

Also by MC Chamberlain
ARMSMAN SERIES
Ghosted - Book IV

<u>*AVAILABLITY TBD*</u>

A man no one can find is a man most dangerous. He can lurk in the open, waiting to do what he must, what he enjoys, whenever desired to whoever gets in the way.

The Families, the hateful Fathers, his own government, and Church want Stone dead. Mafia hitmen want him for money and bragging rights. Anyone, even a common man on the street, can try to take Stone down. If anyone can live to tell the tale, rich rewards are on Stone's head.

But there is nowhere to hide for a man like Stone in the technology of the 23rd century. The powerful Church knows everything. In shadows filled with eyes and ears, Stone cannot slither away. No one can be trusted, sometimes even those closest.

Solution: Become a Ghost. Stone's scruffy techno-wizard joins the minds of the two most powerful AI's, turning a Stone into a ghostly fog. The more anyone looks for Stone, the further away he sinks into the ghost world. Armsman Stone can hide from the entire universe.

But can he hide from the cost?

Can he hide from who he is, a natural-born killer?'

Join Stones Retirement Club to receive word when Armsman Stone's adventures hit the shelves and other new

work just for you. Go to mcchamberlain.com/stone. You will receive 3 FREE prequels (ebooks 90K+ Words).

Armsman Stone's adventures hit the shelves and other new work just for you. Go to mcchamberlain.com/stone. You will receive 3 FREE prequels (ebooks 90K+ Words).

There are stories that span days, years, and even centuries. This story is told by the last Earth Human spans millennia. The end of Earth's Humanity came and went in an unnoticed moment of infinite time.

In the year 2090, Selene Sofia Sanna died in the arms of her lover. 2000 years later, powerful forces with hidden motives resurrected Selene to begin the story of a mortal man destined to battle Hate, the man she fell in love with. With a longing heart, Selene tells of the fall of Mother Earth by the relentless, hateful Father's Empire. She tells of the dreadful deaths of billions of innocent lives and of her true love, the self-centered man with no conscience, selected from Earth Humanity to one day defend Love from Hate in the only way possible; Battle evil with more evil.

Can Resurrected Selene's love for her man one day bring him back?

Follow along with Selene as she begins the story of the last Armsman.

Stone bullies his way onto the last ship escaping the End of Earth.

Facing certain death in hard space, he tells of his return to the life of his youth after being dishonorably released from the elite Special Armed Services.

Alone without allies, where else could a cold-hearted killer go?

The Family embraced him as a lost child. Assignment after assignment, Stone does what he knows how to do. Take out the human garbage in his way, without feeling, without hesitation.

When Stone pulls the trigger, a new hellish nightmare haunts him.

Something tickles his hard heart. He is awakening from the nightmares.

Stone meets a Greek goddess. She falls in love with him. She sees a glimmer of redemption waking in a heart made of Hate.

After all, love covers many sins, but could it cover Stones?

Meanwhile, powerful forces are watching, keeping Stone alive at great cost.

If Stone survives to reach Saturn Station, he could start again.

Can he escape Hate before Love Awakens the last Armsman?

FREE EBOOK

Join Stones Retirement Club to receive word when Armsman Stone's adventures hit the shelves and other new work just for you. Go to mcchamberlain.com/stone. You will receive 3 FREE prequels (ebooks 90K+ Words).

ABOUT

MC (Max) Chamberlain is an emerging author of sci-fi thrillers-operas.

Max loves cats. If Max had his wish, an entire universe somewhere out there should be just for cats. Galaxies full of worlds populated by cays. Entire worlds of play toys, cat treats and, of course, islands of sandboxes. To be far, a Universe for dogs to balance nature should also exit.

Often you can find pictures of Max's two cats on Instagram and Facebook. Occasionally, he posts about travels around Florida where he enjoys no snow.

Max grew up watching black and white TV. Moon landings, Carl Sagan, Captain Kirk and a telescope under heavenly skies full of mysterious stars stirred his young imagination. Since those freezing cold nights he has asked the question, "Are we alone?"

Max thinks he retired after 30 years in IT services. Two cats, one dog, a wonderful wife, grand kids and an imagination for adventures of characters like Stone, Princess Eden, Agent Torres and the mysterious Queen Princess Rorena keep him awake at nights.

facebook.com/mcmaxchamberlain

instagram.com/fussputter

tiktok.com/@mcmaxchamberlain

threads.net/@fussputter

EXTRA

The Ahhavian huddled close, their energy massing into one cloud the size of a billion stars. They heard humankind groan. They heard the angry whinny of their pets, the Seabra.

Strapped to their sides, they carried tools of war. Swords and shields, spears as energy thunderbolts. In wagons, they brought energy cannons and devices so powerful said to destroy worlds. Toys of war they learned of and found lying all about the greater nothingness, just as if children scattered them in disinterest. Most of all, they carried their love. It was something they found when they were human. Now, they were powerful. With love, they could defeat humankind's hate for one another. They would bestow lasting peace on humankind everywhere. Then, they, the patient Ahhavian, would finally become immortals as the many gods.

Glorious victory was assured. Who can stand against us, they sang. We will save humankind for all time, they exclaimed.

Just as they crested the last cluster of newly birthed galaxies, they drew their wagons and war horses to a stop. What they saw with energy eyes quieted their songs of victory. They looked at each other with sadness. They feared for humankind. They feared for their own existence.

The All Gods enjoyed a good war.